"A stunning debut co
in all its terrifying permutations.
all have known or have been, rendered with unflinching
honesty but also with compassion and wit." —Nino Ricci

"With her sharpshooter eye and intrepid heart, Katie
Boland is the love child of Dorothy Parker and Jack
Kerouac. In this, her debut collection, her stories and
those who populate them live at the edges of what is civi-
lized: they gamble love and truth, and in reading them,
we cannot help but do the same. *Eat Your Heart Out* is a
title as much as it is a dare." —Claudia Dey

"In this radiantly written collection, Katie Boland tunnels
into the beating, mysterious heart of human connections.
Pummelled by life and haunted with hope, her characters
are so vivid and alive, you'd swear they're right behind
you. Astonishing." —Caroline Leavitt, *New York Times*
best-selling author of *Pictures of You*

EAT YOUR HEART OUT

KATIE BOLAND

BRINDLE
& GLASS

Brindle & Glass Publishing Ltd.
brindleandglass.com

LIBRARY AND ARCHIVES CANADA CATALOGUING IN PUBLICATION
Boland, Katie, 1988–
Eat your heart out / Katie Boland.

Short stories.
Issued also in electronic formats.
ISBN 978-1-926972-93-0

I. Title.

PS8603.O452E28 2013   C813'.6   C2012-907615-5

Editor: Lynne Van Luven
Proofreader: Heather Sangster, Strong Finish
Interior photography: Katie Boland
Design and cover illustration: Pete Kohut
Author photo: Gail Harvey

Brindle & Glass is pleased to acknowledge the financial support for its publishing
program from the Government of Canada through the Canada Book Fund, Canada
Council for the Arts, and the Province of British Columbia through the British
Columbia Arts Council and the Book Publishing Tax Credit.

The interior pages of this book have been printed on 30% post-consumer
recycled paper, processed chlorine free, and printed with vegetable-based inks.

1 2 3 4 5 17 16 15 14 13

PRINTED IN CANADA

To sweet Peter,
It was the broken heart you gave me (and that I gave me) that told me to start writing.
And, to Amy, my eternal optimist.

Contents

1   Tragic Hero

37   Sweetieface

59   Forever Ago

65   The Falling Action

87   Swelter

99   Monster

109 Saturday

135 Gun Shy

159 The Way We Were

187 Mama

231 Acknowledgments
232 About the Author

Tragic Hero

I met Maggie Dunlappy when she was seventeen and a half years old.

She reminded me of Scarlett O'Hara. You know how they describe her in that book? She wasn't beautiful, but men rarely noticed because of her personality. Maggie wasn't a real looker, but once you got looking at her you couldn't tell anymore.

It was her eyes. Too close together, but they were goddamn beautiful if you took the time to notice. They were this bright blue and they sparkled at you, whether she wanted them to or not. I watched a lot of men fall into those eyes. Maggie'd say, "Hello," all sweet and innocentlike, and I would think, Man overboard! Another one drowned! Poor bastards.

She had these pretty lips. Pink, pretty lips. And you got the impression that she knew how to use them. She didn't have a real elegance to her, you get my drift?

And she had this dyed red hair. It was brassy as shit; she never did it right. You could always see the colours from before peeking out. She said she liked it that way, that the colours reminded her of where she'd been. Used to drive me nuts.

She always wore blue jeans, and a showy type of top. She said her mom had always been like that. Said it was womanlike. That drove me nuts too.

Yeah, she wasn't sophisticated, but there was something really charming about her. Don't get the wrong impression, though.

There wasn't any monkey business. I liked her like I wanted to help her out or something. She didn't ask, but I just wanted to.

And I think she liked me too.

I was forty-four at the time, but I looked good, I don't think she could tell.

No, she couldn't tell. No way, and I never told her.

I have basically worked at every goddamn paper across this country. I worked in Chicago, in New York, in Florida, even Alaska. I ended up in this nowhere town, where there are three churches and one volunteer fire station, because people hate to be told the truth. I should be writing for *The New York Times,* but talent is a projection that dissolves when you piss too many people off.

I drink at the bar down the street from the paper. I usually sit alone. I don't have a problem with it.

Actually, I prefer it.

I was having my daily beers. I think I was on the third one, so I was feeling loose but hadn't heard the click in my head yet. The click tells me it's time to stop, time to go home. Some days that click is harder to get than others. This day the click was being a real mother.

I was reading a book when I met her, *The Sun Also Rises* or something like that. I only read the classics. There's too much shit people read today, that's why they are so stupid. Makes me real sick when I get to thinking about it, so I'll change the subject now.

Anyway, I'm reading this book, and out of the corner of my eye I see this young thing walking toward me. I think to myself, She's not bad. Half-decent minus the hair but too young for me. What's more, I'm not looking to talk to anybody. I decide that if she comes up here I'm telling her to take a hike.

But sure as hell she walks right up to me. In retrospect, I figure she thought that me looking at her was me giving the go-ahead.

"Hi. Are you sitting alone?"

"Yeah. I mean, no. I mean, yeah, I'm sitting alone, but I'm fine." I gave her this real tight smile, like "You can get along now" type thing. They say facial expressions are ninety percent of human communication. It's true, let me tell you. But Maggie was always real bad at reading that stuff.

"Oh! I'm alone too. It seems silly to sit side by side at two empty tables if we're both here alone. So I'll just sit right here."

She lifts her hands like she's shrugging when she says that, all innocent, like "Oh! Look at this! A spot for me, just right here!" Like she didn't plan it out. Fat fucking chance. I saw her coming a mile way.

"Listen, sweetheart, you're nice and everything, but I'm busy right now."

Then I turn back to my book, figuring she'll be on her way.

But half a page later I look up and she's sat her ass right down.

"Was I speaking Swahili?"

"No."

"I don't want you here."

Then she looks at me, real calm, with those sparkly blue eyes, and says, "I don't remember asking."

She was a pistol like that. I wasn't expecting her to say something like that.

"I like sitting with someone," she goes.

I look at her, exasperated, and make a big show of going back to my book.

But I couldn't focus, knowing those two sparkly eyes were just staring at me. It was like they were burning holes in my head.

Finally, I put my book down on the table with a big flourish.

I looked around for another table. Some Mexican couple had just taken the last one. Just my typical luck.

So then I stare at her in total silence for about a minute, trying to scare her away. But she just stares right back. I respected her for that.

"Okay, miss, if you aren't going to let me read, talk."

Then she smiles at me real pleased, like she just loved talking.

"Oh, great! Okay, well my name is Maggie Dunlappy. What's yours?"

"I'm Rich." Then I looked her up and down. "How old are you?"

She leaned over the table, as if she was telling me a secret. Thanks to her showy top I saw a lot more than I wanted to. You get the idea.

"I'm seventeen and a half, but I lied and told the bartender I was twenty-three." Then she pushes her shoulders back like she's proud of herself. "Do you think I pass?"

"No."

"Oh."

I looked up toward the ceiling for a lot of the time after that. I didn't want her to think I was getting fresh.

"Sorry, kid, you look about nineteen tops. I wouldn't even give you a go and you're not half bad."

She looked like she didn't know if I was complimenting or insulting her, but she recovered quick.

"So tell me about yourself, Rich. Are you married? Do you have kids or anything?"

"Did you rehearse that one?"

She said no, all serious and confused, like why would anyone rehearse something like that?

"I don't believe in marriage and I don't believe in children. No offence on the second count," I answered.

She looked like she didn't quite know what I meant and was scared to ask. Then she put on this real sweet smile.

"Really? A nice man like you not married?"

"I was married once. A lot of others have wanted to marry me, but the rule is that I stay for dinner, not for breakfast."

She starts laughing, like I'm a real comedian. I swear to Christ, she laughed at me for about five minutes, like I was killing her, like I just couldn't be serious. I wait for a couple of minutes, like any normal comedian would. Maybe she just thinks I'm funny or something, I don't know. But then it dawns on me.

She isn't laughing at me because I told a funny joke. She's laughing at me because I *am* the funny joke.

Then I get kind of mad: who's this young thing to be laughing at me and ruining my drink, you know?

"What? Why are you laughing like that?"

Then she looks at me with good intentions, just good intentions, and this real sweetness and understanding. Her eyes get big and blue, and she stops laughing. "You're a real pisser, aren't you?"

Something changed after she said that. She was as tall as a shotgun and just as noisy.

I got to know Maggie pretty quick. Mostly on account of her love for talking, but also because I would watch her. She showed up at the bar every night. I saw her so often that I couldn't help but like her.

She had this vibe of being alone. Didn't matter if she was in a bar full of people, she always seemed alone. Even when she was sitting across from me at the table she looked alone. It was her face. Her face was a lonely sight.

There is something goddamn tragic about a lonely-looking young person. Looks wrong. I called her on it. In a sensitive-type way, of course.

"What the hell are you doing alone at this bar?"

"I'm with you."

"You know what I mean, showing up alone. Don't you have friends?"

"Yeah."

I looked at her, expecting her to carry on like usual. But she didn't. She just looked around the bar, sipping her vodka-soda.

I stuck my hand out in the middle of the table and made a summoning-type motion at her, like "Tell me more." I near gave myself carpal tunnel doing all that summoning before she finally caught on. She was wearing a real showy shirt that night, and I kept trying to stare at her eyebrows.

"Oh! Yeah, I have friends. I have lots of friends back home. I've just been moving around a lot lately. I've only been here for like six months, and . . . oh, you don't want to hear it."

"I asked you, didn't I?"

She laughed. I was always making her laugh. She thought I was so smart and I could tell she wished she knew more people like me.

"Okay. Well, I had this boyfriend, and I really liked him, you know? And—and then, well, I don't know what changed, I thought he really loved me too, and . . ."

Out of nowhere she started crying. And Maggie's crying never started slow and built up, like a normal person's. She went from smiling to full-out woman-hysterics bawling.

So, I was sitting there, at the bar with her, and she was just crying her guts out. Everyone was looking at me like I'm the bad guy, like I must be breaking this young thing's heart or something.

I looked to all the other patrons. "We're not together!"

"Oh, that's great, Rich!"

I hate it when women cry. I hear these alarm bells go off in my head, saying, "Make it stop! Make it stop!" In my life, I've done near everything to make a woman stop crying. If I had a dime for every lie I told to make a woman stop crying, I'd be a millionaire, believe you me. So I did to Maggie what I always do when I'm telling a woman something I want her to believe. I started to pat her hand, real slow and convincing.

And she looked at me after a couple of pats, thankful, like I'm some knight in shining armor.

"I'm sorry, Rich." She took a bar napkin I had given her and blew her nose so loud that anyone who wasn't already looking at us could start. "This is why I didn't want to talk about it."

Knowing better than to engage in conversation with an emotional woman, I said, "Don't worry, we don't have to . . ."

But before I could get my sentence out, she carried on like all crying women do; fast and like I care.

"I just really loved him, you know? His name was Jared, and one day I noticed he started to look at me different. We were living together at that point—"

"What the Christ are you doing living with someone at your age?"

"Rich, a seventeen-year-old girl is the same maturity as a thirty-year-old man. That's a literal fact."

"Oh for fuck's . . . from where? *Bullshitter's Digest*?"

"Can I finish my story, please?"

I nodded begrudgingly.

"So, we were living together, and I didn't know what to do. I would just try to be nicer and nicer to him. But the nicer I was, the less he wanted anything to do with me. I don't know what I did wrong. Then he kicked me out, said he met someone new. I know who too. She's this trashy, fat, blond girl. That made it way worse. It was like I bugged him so much that he was willing to date a fat girl just to get away from me."

She had a point there.

"And I was new to town when we got together, so all of his friends became my friends. That was stupid of me. Now his friends don't want anything to do with me either. It's just been sad because I guess he never meant anything he said."

Then she looked at me like she couldn't believe that someone would ever say something they didn't mean.

"Well, yeah, that's people for you," I said. "Let me tell you something."

She stopped crying for a moment and perked up.

"People are always saying shit they don't mean."

"Really?"

"Yes. I hate to break it to you, but you can't trust anyone. Just your own self."

"How do you know?"

"I've had my heart broken too."

This piqued her interest. "Who was she?"

"Her name was Rosemary. I was a little older than you when we got together but not much."

"Was this the woman you were married to?"

I forgot I'd told her that. Took me off centre a little.

"Uh, well, yes." I shrugged when I said that. Don't know why.

"What happened?"

I felt myself wanting to tell her what happened.

"Hey, we are talking about you. Not me."

"You can tell me." She inched forward and put her hand on my hand now, like she was comforting me. I moved away fast.

"Well, what happened was, it didn't work out."

She let her straw fall out of her mouth, and her lips went into this pretty pout. She did look charming, even with makeup all over her face.

"Trust me, you get sick of being the good guy."

She got real quiet after I said that. Then she goes, "You sound like my dad" in such a way that I took it as a compliment.

"Your dad must be a pretty smart guy then."

She kept sipping her drink.

"I don't know him really."

"What do you mean?"

"He left about five years ago. I haven't seen him in a year or so. Not since I left home. And before he left, he was in and out. Mainly out. I really just know what my mom told me he thought about stuff. Sounds kind of like you."

Then she shrugged and looked down, back to sipping her drink.

I felt really bad for her. It made me think I could tell her stuff. Tell her things he should have told her. See? That's where the charity part came in.

"Don't trust people," I said.

She pushed her drink to the middle of the table. She interlaced her little fingers, making a fist, and rested it on the marked wood between us.

"That's a sad way to be."

I was surprised by her saying something so blunt to me.

"Who's the one crying here?"

"Yeah, I'm crying this time, but lately, at night, I think about how next time it'll be different. It'll work out. Because I'll make the new guy I'm with happy too. As happy as Jared made me."

"No one is going to make you happy." I said, and I meant it.

Then she looked away, real wistful, like what I was telling her was hurting. She took her lip gloss out and put too much on.

Fleetwood Mac's "Landslide" started playing at the bar, and she turned to me, all excited and drunk, how young women get, and said, "Oh! I love this song! This is my favourite song!"

I looked at her, tipsy myself, and I remembered something I had forgotten for a long time.

"It was Rosemary's too."

It's strange sensation, remembering something that you forgot a long time ago. It reminds you of a lot of other stuff you used to know too.

Pretty soon, three days a week, she got to meeting me after work for dinner. I told everybody she was my niece from out of town. I didn't want them thinking anything was going on. None of them seemed to remember that I was an only child.

I didn't mind taking Maggie out. Not if I didn't have anything better to do. I started taking her to the bigger city down the way.

"You know, Maggie, you shouldn't chew with your mouth open. It's unladylike."

She closed her mouth real quick and covered her lips with her hand. She was disarming like that. She never got embarrassed, so I never felt bad for helping her.

She swallowed.

"So what's this called?" She took her chopsticks and pointed at a plate across from her.

"A spicy tuna roll."

"Spicy? Is it hot?"

"Just try it."

"What if it's too hot?"

"Just try it, Maggie. You should expose yourself to new things."

"Why?"

"It'll make you more well rounded."

"Oh."

She said "Oh," like she accepted that she had no idea what I meant, and like it didn't bother her. She had low expectations for herself. I didn't like it.

"You should ask me what I meant by well rounded, Maggie."

She sighed. "What did you mean by well rounded?"

"I meant it will make you a more . . . a more fulfilled and a more exposed . . . a more . . ."

She started laughing at me.

"Let me finish."

"Sorry."

"It will make you a more educated person."

"Like you?" She rolled her eyes and threw a piece into her mouth, chewing suspiciously. After a few seconds, she got this big grin on her face.

I got a real kick out of that.

"So what'd you do today, missy?"

"Oh, just regular stuff, cleaning and everything. This afternoon I looked around for another job. I just hate the restaurant and they aren't giving me enough hours. And then I hung around the place I'm staying and I don't know, waited for you to be done work. What about you?"

"Oh, nothing really. I interviewed the mayor about his plans for building that new highway, wrote about that for a bit."

She looked like I had interviewed Jesus himself.

"You interviewed the mayor? Are you shitting me?"

"No. I'm not 'shitting' you."

"Wow, Rich! I can't believe it!"

"That guy's a liar and a crook."

"But he is famous! You interviewed the mayor! I am so jealous. It must be so much fun to have such an exciting job like that. You must just love getting out of bed every day."

I spilt some soy sauce down my tie.

"Yeah, that's what everybody thinks."

"You don't like it?"

"Not really, no."

"Why not?"

"Because I spend my life writing about everything bad that happens in the world. Or about all the liars who tell people they can fix everything bad. I work with a bunch of jackasses who can't write their way out of a wet paper bag."

"You practise that or something?" she said and laughed, all proud of herself. God, she thought she was funny sometimes.

"You can't use my own lines on me. It's unoriginal."

I took my napkin and dipped it in water, hoping to get the stain out. I was ferocious with my movements.

"If I had known what the paper would be like going in, I never would've taken the job," I told her.

"Really?"

"Yeah."

"Well, what would you rather do?"

"Scrub toilets."

"I'm serious!"

"I don't know, kid. Write books. Be the next Ernest Hemingway."

"Is he famous?"

"A bit."

"Why don't you write books?"

"When you get older you'll know it's not that simple."

"Why not?"

"You ask a lot of questions."

"Sorry." She reached out, asking for my tie. I took it off and gave it to her. She dipped her napkin in water.

"No, it's just . . . life has a funny way of surprising you. You point it in one direction, and before you know it, it's taken off so far that way that you can't turn it back."

She looked at me blankly. I wasn't sure if she understood what I meant. I opened my mouth to tell her more of what grown-ups know, but she butted right in, spinning her own yarn, never looking at me, just cleaning my tie.

"That was like this one time just after I moved out on my own. Money was real tight, and I was working at this shoe shop. But the owner was this mean old man, a pervert. All I wanted to do was quit and get another job, but I couldn't because I had to pay rent, I had to eat. No choice. So I stayed 'til someone else would hire me. Took a long time, me being so young and stuff. But I got through it."

I stayed quiet for a second after she said that.

"What does that have to do with what I just said?"

"Oh! Probably nothing. That was stupid of me. I just thought, Two bad situations you didn't see coming, you know?"

"Oh, yeah, I see what you mean." I lied. To this day I have no idea what she was getting at. She was a little loopy like that, drawing parallels, seeing herself in other people.

"Do you like the people you work with at least? Even if they aren't all smart like you?" she asked.

"Think about what you just asked me."

She did, still cleaning my tie. She thought about it so hard that eventually I had to interrupt her thinking and answer my own goddamn question.

"I meant, if they were stupid, how could I like them?"

"Oh! Oh, I get it!"

"You must feel the same about dumb people, you're smart."

"I'm not smart."

"Yes, you are."

"You think so?" She looked up at me for a brief moment.

"What do you mean? No one calls you smart?"

"No, not really. I mean, I didn't do great in school and my mom never called me smart, and you know about my dad, so, no. Not really."

"Well, you are damn smart, and don't you let anyone tell you different."

She shrugged.

"What are your parents like?" she asked.

"I didn't really know my dad. He died when I was young, he was kind of a drunk, you know? I figure I was better growing up without him. And my mom's fine. She means well, she's just . . . clueless, you know?"

"Oh?" She handed me back my tie. The stain was gone.

"She reads my columns, or she tries to. She calls me up about them, but most of the time I just think, What's the point? I don't see why she tries, you know?"

"Because she loves you, probably."

"Yeah, probably. Just feels futile."

"What does futile mean?"

"Pointless."

"Futile . . ."

"Try to use it in a sentence tomorrow." I got back to the point I was making. "My largest regret is that my childhood was unnecessarily lonely and I blame my mother for that."

"I hope that's not true for my baby."

"What do you mean *your* baby?"

"I really want to have a baby."

"Now?"

"Yeah, I would."

"Don't you dare get knocked up for a good ten years. Can you imagine you having a baby? You are a goddamn baby."

"No, I know . . . but I'd be a good mom, I know I would. I'd love my baby so much."

"It's a lot harder that it seems, kid."

She looked at me like I was just ridiculous. "How do you know?"

She tilted her head down and I got a good look at that dog's breakfast.

"You should really get your hair dyed—"

She interrupted. "So, since Rosemary? Was it Rosemary?"

"What's she got to do with this?"

"No, nothing. Just since her, no serious women?"

"No. No, not really." I ripped my nail to the quick.

"Wow."

"Why are you always saying wow, kid? It makes you seem dumber than you are." It was mean I said that to her, but my nail really hurt. I hid it under the table. "I've never wanted to be committed."

"Not with anyone? Not ever?"

"No. I get committed, goodbye freedom. Why would I want that?"

She looked away and I went back to eating. When I thought the conversation was over, she got back to talking.

"I was at Starbucks this one time, this reminds me of that. You know how Starbucks has those quote things on the back of their cups? Well, there was this one quote, and it went like, it went something like, 'the irony . . .' irony . . . is that right?"

"Could be. I don't know what you're talking about yet."

"Oh. Okay, well, I think it's irony . . . anyway, 'The irony of commitment is that it's ultimately freeing.'"

I laughed real hard at that one. "That would be ironic, yes."

"Don't laugh, this is good! Just listen, okay?"

I nodded my head. I always did listen to her, more than I did other people. Don't know why.

"It said like 'When you commit to something, it frees you of the doubts in your head.' I don't know, something like that. That always stuck with me. I think it's true."

When she gave me that spiel, she looked real hopeful. But it was this terrifying hope around her eyes. Really, it scared me. I hadn't seen that kind of hope from anyone in so long that I had to set her straight.

"You know why you only see shit like that written on Starbucks cups?"

"No, why?"

"Because the only people stupid enough to believe that bullshit are the same idiots who are willing to pay five dollars for a goddamn coffee."

She laughed real hard at that. But when she laughed it was a sad laugh. She looked like she'd been woken up from a dream.

"You're probably right."

She smiled at me, with this smile coloured blue. I wondered then if maybe she wanted to stay dreaming.

"Should I get the cheque, kid?" I asked her.

"Sure," she said. "Sure."

A couple of months passed like that. We would go to dinner, then get a few drinks, but around eleven-thirty Maggie would always say that she had to go. So I would pay the bill and we would be on our way. I knew she was lying, though. She didn't have anywhere to be.

I could tell she was always nervous about overstaying her welcome. She didn't want me to get sick of her. I would try to make it real obvious that I wasn't sick of her, but she was still nervous. Must have been something she learned because I couldn't shake her out of it. She'd put her arms around herself and shake like she was cold in her ridiculous tops.

"Look at me, cold! I must be tired," and then I'd know it was time to drive her home.

It all changed at three o'clock one morning. When I got the call, I had a woman next to me in bed. A redhead I'd picked up at the bar. I was quiet, careful not to wake her.

"Hello?" I whispered.

"Rich?"

"Maggie?" I knew instantly who it was.

"I'm so sorry, sorry I'm calling this late."

"What's wrong? Are you okay?"

"Yes. Well, no."

Then she started crying hard into the phone.

"Maggie, what's wrong? Tell me what happened."

The woman next to me in bed started tossing.

"Who are you talking to, Rich?"

I shushed her. I was probably too blunt about it, but all I cared about right then was Maggie. I took the phone and moved across the room.

"Maggie, take a deep breath, try to tell me what's wrong."

She took big gulps of air. I had to strain to hear her.

"I just got home from this party, and I just walked in the first room and it's all a mess, I didn't even go in and see anything more. I'm too scared. I don't think he's still in there, but it's so dark and I don't know my neighbours. I just don't know what to do. Should I go back in?"

She started crying real hard again.

"No. Don't go back in, Maggie. It's okay. Here, this is what you do, okay? You get out of there right now. Go to that gas station at the bottom of your street, okay? You wait there, and you stay right next to the guy working there. I'm going to come right now and get you. You got it?"

She was still crying.

"Don't worry. Go to the gas station right now, okay?"

"Yeah, okay."

"I'll be there in ten minutes."

"Okay, bye."

I put the phone down, and the woman in bed was staring at me.

"What happened?" she asked

I started running around, trying to find my pants and a decent shirt.

"My niece called, she had a break-in. So I got to go get her."

"Oh no. Is she okay?"

"Yeah. I hate to do this, but you have your car, right?"

The lady sat up in bed and pulled the covers over her bare chest.

"Yeah?"

"You should probably go home. She has to sleep here tonight."

She sat up even more.

"All right."

She got all her stuff together. Three minutes later I was out the door.

When I picked Maggie up she had stopped crying, but she was wearing this real tiny dress, and she was just shaking from the cold.

I got her into the car. I probably drove too fast, but it threw me off to see her like that. When we got to my place she looked so tiny and so tired. I don't know why, but she looked smaller than she ever did before.

"Here, get changed into this T-shirt and these shorts here," I told her.

"Thanks."

"You take the bed."

"No. I couldn't do that. Not after I woke you and everything."

"Take it."

"Okay."

"I'm just going to sleep on the couch, you call if you need anything," I told her.

About five minutes later she came over to the couch. I wasn't lying down yet, I was sitting up, just thinking about how mad I was that someone would break into her apartment.

"What's up, kid?"

"Oh, nothing. I just can't really sleep, and I heard you out here, so I figured . . . maybe you'd like to talk or something?"

"Yeah, sure. I don't think I'm going to sleep now anyhow."

She came and sat next to me on the couch.

"What a bad night."

"That's fucking awful what happened. We'll get you a better lock and all that tomorrow. Call the police." I felt responsible. Why hadn't I checked her locks before?

"The party sucked too."

"What happened?"

She looked at me like she was happy I asked what happened.

I got the idea that's why she came out to talk. Women are see-through sometimes.

"Well, I knew Jared was going to be there with his new girl. So I was prepared to see them. I got all dolled up, wore that dress. And when I got there he noticed me right away. He was staring at me the whole damn time, I swear. So after about an hour, I went up to say hi to him, you know? Thought I'd be mature, or whatever. But he looked at me like he really hated me. Then right in the middle of him talking to me, he takes his girl's hand and he just walks away. I couldn't believe it. He was so mean. He looked at me like he didn't even know me, Rich. Like he didn't even know me."

"Fuck him. Did you tell him off?"

"No, I spent the whole night crying in the bathroom after that, like a dumb baby."

"You have to start sticking up for yourself, Maggie."

"But I still love him."

"Jesus, Maggie. What you need to do is stop showing people how you feel."

"But I'm not good at hiding how I feel."

"Well, you got to get better at hiding it, kid. You can't go around showing every asshole how much they upset you. Then they think they won."

"What am I supposed to do?"

"You have to act like you don't care."

She put her head in her hands.

"People prey on weakness," I continued. "You can't show them that you're weak. You can only show them that you're strong. You do that by showing them that you don't care."

"You aren't always going to be strong, though," she whispered.

"Who needs to know that?"

She sighed after I said that. She looked so small on my couch. Then a wash of tears came to her eyes, but I could tell she was trying to fight them. I put my arm around her, just instinctively.

"Why are men so mean?" she asked me.

"Listen, every asshole who isn't good enough for you is going to be mean to you because you scare them. You have a lot going for you, kid. You don't need to wear a dress like that to look beautiful. You look beautiful right now, just normal."

"You think I'm beautiful?"

"Yes. I do."

She smiled after I said that. I think it meant a lot to her. And she was beautiful. Well, once you really got looking at her anyway. I thought it was nice of me to be building up her confidence.

"You need to know how much you got going for you, Maggie. Until then, nobody else is going to know."

She moved in closer after I said that. She rested her head on my shoulder.

"Yeah."

Then she went quiet for a bit. I thought maybe she'd fallen asleep.

"Are you mean to women?"

"No. I tell them what I'm like up front. They know what they're getting into."

"They probably fall in love with you anyway, though."

"No. I don't let that happen."

"I bet they all fall in love with you even though they don't want to."

"Well, if they are falling in love with me it's because they really want to, trust me. I make it hard for them to think I'd ever love them back."

"You don't think that's mean?"

"I think that's honest."

She turned her head away when I said that.

"Maybe you're right. Maybe this love thing is stupid."

"See? Now you get it, kid. I knew you would."

I moved my arm from her shoulder. I gave her a few quick pats on the knee. She smiled back at me. A thought struck me.

"What made you come up to me that night at the bar? Why'd you want to talk to me?"

"You looked lonely." Then she said, "I don't know what I would've done without you tonight," as if her previous statement held no weight at all.

I didn't sleep that night. I watched the sunrise the next morning out of my bedroom window.

I've never seen such beautiful colours in my whole goddamn life.

After the break-in, I would take her to see a movie about once a week. I remember because it was around then that I got sick of eating out all the time.

She didn't mind one bit, she loved to go see movies. It made her happier than a cochon in shit. She would tell me all about the movie stars beforehand. I would be praying she'd shut up the whole car ride there. I couldn't tell her to shut up, though. Talking about them made her too happy.

"I really like that other movie Jake Gyllenhaal did."

"Yeah?"

"Yeah, it's called *The Day After Tomorrow*, about this huge weather disaster in the future."

"I can hardly wait for the musical."

"Do you think they'll make a musical?"

"No. I was kidding."

"Oh. Well, you know that's interesting because I think Jake Gyllenhaal would be just great in a musical. He's very physical, you know, I bet you he can dance."

"You don't say."

"He's so handsome too. He'd be able to look masculine while singing. That's hard to do. He definitely isn't gay. He used to date Kirsten Dunst, you know that?"

"Nope."

"Yeah, he did. And all my friends say that she's an ugly slag, but I think she's kind of cute. She has crooked teeth like mine. And I've always thought mine were kind of cute."

"They are."

She beamed after I said that. I never knew I could be such a charitable guy.

"Sorry to change the subject, kid, because I am just riveted."

"You don't need to lie."

"I was only kidding."

"Go on, change the subject."

"Did you find that necklace stolen in the break-in? The one your mom gave you?"

"Oh, no. I didn't. I'm pretty sure it's gone."

"Ah, shit."

"No big deal. It was just a little gold heart on a chain. It had sentimental value because my dad gave it to my mom."

"You notice anything else they took?"

"No, it was a big joke on them. I don't have anything worth taking."

"Yeah, well, good. Sick fucks."

"Some might say it was 'ironic.'"

I laughed.

The movie that night was awful. I had bought her this big popcorn. She was eating it so goddamn loud it was like listening to a pig eating celery, I swear to you.

"Can you chew with your mouth closed?"

She looked at me, real pissy, then she closed her mouth and turned away from me. I figured she must have been on her rag or something.

Then about five minutes later, when I was finally starting to follow the movie, she says, real loud, "You should write a book, you know that?"

I looked at her like she was crazy. "Why?"

"Because you think you know everything."

She turned back away from me after she said it and didn't look at me again for the whole movie. She was crazier than a shithouse rat, but she really knew how to make a point, I'll give her that.

Yeah, she could really make a point.

Over the next couple of weeks I found it real hard to focus at work. I would be writing a story, or interviewing some person, and Maggie would just pop into my head. I'd think of something she said, or some funny look she gave me, and I'd lose whatever was happening in front of me.

Not like I minded, though. Sometimes I liked the break it gave my mind from everything familiar.

Familiarity will kill a man quicker than cancer, believe me.

She turned eighteen late that spring. I told her I'd take her out, and she said something bashful like I didn't have to. That it wasn't that big a deal.

I wanted to. Eighteen is a big deal. You make it that far it's something to celebrate.

I remember my eighteenth birthday like yesterday. I remember being alone and wishing I had my dad to take me out. I didn't tell her that, though. I made some joke that we needed to celebrate her entrance into adulthood and misery. And she laughed, but I could tell that she was excited. I think she was wanting to put everything behind her.

I picked her up at her place at around seven o'clock.

I remember her walking out of her apartment. I have this clear mental picture of her walking down those stairs.

She was wearing this beautiful blue dress. I think she bought it special for that night because I'd never seen it before. It wasn't showy, just real simple, classy even. It held her at her waist. It made her look graceful. And she had her hair up in this special way that I'd never seen before. It was like Grace Kelly did it sometimes, or how some ladies have it on their wedding day. She wore this bright red lipstick. And in that blue dress her eyes looked bigger and bluer than ever before. I'll never forget how she looked, not for as long as I live.

"You really look like a woman tonight," I told her as she walked to the car.

"Well, thank you, old man."

"I'm not old."

"You're a little old."

"You're catching up."

She looked pleased after I said that. She wanted to be older. She wanted to be something different.

I took her to dinner at this French place that I'd taken a couple of ladies before. They'd all liked it, so I figured that Maggie would too. I kept ordering us glasses of red, and we were both drinking pretty fast.

Halfway through dinner I figured it was time I give her the present. I was tipsy and I remember feeling extremely excited. Bizarre.

I handed the little box across. She looked at it, frozen.

"Rich! You didn't have to get me anything!" She always squealed when she was drunk.

"Of course I did. Eighteen comes once in a lifetime."

"Rich . . . you better not have spent a lot of money on this."

"Don't worry, kid."

Then she moved her little hands and opened the box. It was wrapped in red wrapping paper, I remember, because I asked them to wrap it special. She tore the paper off, just ripped it like a little gypsy.

Then she opened the little blue box. I remember her face looked like it melted.

"Oh my God, Rich."

All I wanted right then was for her to like it.

"Do you like it?"

Then she looked up at me, and her eyes got misty, but in a different way than I'd seen before. Like she'd just witnessed something unreal happen, not sad or anything. Not happy either.

"Rich, I love it."

She took the necklace and brought it close to her face, studying it.

"Does it look like the one that got stolen?"

"Exactly. Exactly the same."

"Really?"

"Yes."

I was pleased as punch—I'd gone all through the department

stores two towns over, trying really hard to find one that matched what she said her mom's had looked like.

Then she put the necklace down on the table. She just stared at me, like I was some painting in a museum or something.

"What?"

"It's just . . ."

"What?"

She went quiet. Then she looked away from me and her face got all scrunched together. She slowly turned back to me, with this expression that I couldn't read.

"No one has ever been as nice to me as you are."

I didn't really know what to say so I just smiled.

"Thanks, kid." And we both smiled at each other for a while after that. But then I think she got nervous somewhere in the middle of the smile. You know the nervous feeling you get when you are staring at someone and they are staring back? I think she got that feeling.

When she got nervous she would always say something real common, or make some stupid joke about herself.

"Rich, I'm shitfaced."

Then the waiter came by and I ordered some more wine.

From that point on I don't remember much. We did end up at my place, I'm sure of that.

Maggie was real gone at that point. Truth is, I was just as gone as she was. I don't know how because she was so much smaller than me, but that girl could really hold her liquor. I liked that about her.

So we were back at my apartment. The room was spinning type thing. You get my drift.

And I remember as soon as we got there, Maggie went to go get herself a glass of water from the kitchen. She tripped on nothing and fell on her little ass halfway there. She blamed her high heels.

I was lying on my couch, facing the ceiling.

"Maggie, I got a song that I just have to play for you."

"Is it good?"

"No, it's awful. That's why I'm playing it for you. I'm not going to play you a shit song on your birthday, kid."

"You can't call me kid anymore. I'm an adult now."

"Okay, woman."

She smiled.

"Yeah, I like that."

She said she liked that real decisive. Her eyes narrowed and she pointed at me when she said it. She was saying it a specific way. She was getting at something, I'm certain.

Anyway, I went to my CD player, and I found this disc an old flame had made me.

It was this cover of Bowie's "Let's Dance," this real slow version, acoustic almost. The guy singing it had this real simple, honest voice. Bowie's version isn't pretty or anything, but when you listen to this guy, you really hear the poetry.

Looking back, I really don't know why I was so dead set on playing it.

I put the song on and then I moved to the couch and I sat right next to her. I didn't realize how dark it was until I sat down.

The acoustic guitar started very slow. It sank into us both.

She moved closer to me and said something like "Oh, Rich! This is so beautiful."

But she said it real quiet, like she wanted to keep listening.

I remember my body sagged closer to hers.

Then she put her hand on my thigh, and she said, "Rich, this is such a beautiful song."

I wanted to be closer to her. I should've sent her home right then, but I didn't. I just wanted to be closer to her. I put my hand on hers. She was so small. I put my other hand on her thigh. I could feel the silk in her dress under my hands.

I could feel her move closer and press up against me. I could smell the alcohol on her. Her skin was so soft and so perfect. I could hear her breathing.

Then I kissed her. Just out of nowhere, just for no reason, just because honest to God I wanted to. I just kissed her. I put my lips on hers, real soft and real tender. I still remember how her lips felt. They were lush and expectant. I swear to you she was expecting it.

But I kissed her first. And that's about as clear as I can make it.

She pulled back away from me, so fast.

"What the fuck are you doing, Rich?"

Then I opened my eyes, and I saw her looking at me with this mix of anger and fear. I'd never seen somebody look equal parts angry and afraid ever before in my life, but her eyes looked real scared. I felt so bad when I saw those eyes.

"I'm sorry, Maggie. I'm sorry. I'm shitfaced and—"

"You are unbelievable!"

"Maggie, I didn't mean it, I just wasn't thinking. Maggie, calm down, I'm sorry—"

She was real drunk, just trying to get her purse and her jacket.

"Maggie, no, don't leave."

"Of course I'm leaving!"

"Maggie, just calm down."

"You're a stupid asshole!"

She was looking at me like she was real shocked that I kissed her. Like she just couldn't believe it.

"Maggie, come on. It's not like you weren't wanting it."

That's where I really messed up. She went off after that.

"Wanting it? Are you out of your mind? You know what you are, Rich? And you listen to me, you know what you are?"

"No, and you can calm right down."

"You know what you are?"

"Maggie, you can lower your voice."

"You are a fucking coward."

"Maggie, I'm just drunk. I didn't mean anything by it—"

"Rich, I was your friend."

"I wasn't trying to ruin it, Maggie. Just calm down."

"Did you think I was going to fuck you?"

I stayed quiet. I didn't know what I thought.

"You are tragic."

I remember being mad after she said that. Real mad.

"Get the fuck out of here, Maggie."

Then she looked at me like I was despicable. I have never seen that type of hate in a woman's eyes before.

"Don't try and pretend like you're kicking me out of here."

She slammed the door and then she was gone.

I lay back down on my couch and stared at the ceiling again.

I swear, I thought she was wanting it too.

I didn't call her the next day.

I kept thinking that I would, but then I just didn't. I kept telling myself I was going to call, but I didn't. Surprised myself with that one.

A couple of days passed. She didn't call me either. So I stopped feeling bad and I just got real mad. I knew I'd made a mistake, but the stuff she said was out of line. And who was she to say all that to me after everything I'd done, you know?

She could pretend she wasn't asking for it, but she was. Then she just got scared. That's what happened. I know I did wrong, but I was drunk. She did some wrong too, she just didn't want to admit it. Women are always being like that.

I went to the bar a few days later, not hoping I'd see her or anything, just to get a drink. Barkeep told me she hadn't been in for about a week or so. I didn't care. It's not like I was looking for her.

One night I picked up this blonde at the bar. I'd known the lady for a little while and she was always making eyes at me, but when I was sitting with Maggie I'd ignore her. I wasn't reading and definitely felt like talking.

"Hi there," she said.

"Hi," I said back.

"I seen you around here. Where's your little girlfriend?"

"She wasn't my girlfriend."

"Daughter?"

"You're being smart." There was no fucking way I looked old enough to be Maggie's dad.

"Yeah, I am."

"My niece."

"Mind if I join you?"

"Not at all."

She sat across from me. I knew where it was going from the moment we started talking. But when I was sitting across from this blonde, staring at her mug, a part of me was wishing I was sitting with Maggie.

After a few beers, I guess I didn't mind so much.

"So this is your place, huh?"

"Yeah."

The blonde looked worse out of the bar. Her face was more wrinkled than I'd thought, and her body had real thickness in the middle. But I was pretty drunk, and beggars just can't be choosers.

"It's nice."

"Not really."

"No, it's nicer than my place."

"Well, that says something."

"What?"

"Nothing. Do you want another drink?"

The lady looked at me real salacious. I knew she did not need another drink.

So we got down to business, you get my drift? But I just wasn't enjoying it. I wasn't enjoying it at all. I don't know if it was the booze, or the lady, but I couldn't stop seeing Maggie's face every time I closed my eyes.

And it wasn't like I was seeing her in a sexual way. I was seeing that face she gave me that night, staring at me. I couldn't get her out of my head. I think the lady caught on after a couple of minutes.

"You okay?" she asks.

"Yeah, I'm fine, it's just the rubber. I can't . . . I've been drinking, I'm sorry."

I rolled off her; there was no point in keeping going. I couldn't anyway. Not with Maggie's face haunting me like that.

The lady looked disappointed. I should've offered to do something for her, but I couldn't be bothered and about twenty minutes later she left.

I called Maggie. She didn't pick up, so I left her a message.

Her voice sounded different on the message than I remembered, younger or something.

"Hi, kid, it's Rich. Look, I been meaning to call you, and I know I haven't. I just wanted to say I'm sorry. About everything. Call me back and we'll talk about it. Okay, kid?"

Then I hung up, and I felt satisfied, knowing she would call me back.

Maggie did not call me back for a week.

At first I figured, you know, give her a little time. She'll call. Then a little later, I thought, Just give her a little more time. She's just digesting what you said.

But no.

A fucking week passed and not one word from her mouth.

Then I thought, Enough of this bullshit. I was nice enough to call her and apologize, and she can't be bothered to call back.

So I called her again. Only this time, she picked up the phone.

"Yes?" she said, all entitledlike. Almost like a British person or something, with a little accent. She could be snooty when she wanted to.

"It's Rich." I was shocked that she had picked up.

"I know."

Then the phone went silent for a few seconds. I couldn't believe how she was acting.

"I called you."

"Yes, I got the message."

"And . . . ?"

"And I was thinking."

"About what?"

Then she sighed into the phone.

"If I was going to call you back or not, dummy."

"Oh."

Then she went silent again.

"Well, were you?"

"I don't know. I hadn't decided yet." She said that real casual.

"Oh, come on, Maggie. I know I fucked up."

"Yes, you did."

I didn't know what more to say.

"I'm sorry, kid."

I could hear her breathing. I thought she might hang up. I sat there listening to her breathing for a good two minutes. I didn't want to say anything in case she hung up.

Then finally she said, "Okay."

"Okay, what?"

"Okay, I forgive you."

"Really?"

"Yes. You know why?"

"No, why?"

"Because I know you won't let me down again, Rich."

Then she hung up the phone.

We never talked about what happened ever again after that conversation.

She came to the bar that night. Things weren't normal, but we pretended they were. That's how things get back to normal. You just got to pretend until you forget you are pretending, and then things are normal again. That's how it works.

She's twenty-two now.

Around six months ago, she moved. Met some guy when he was here visiting, and they fell in love real fast, and she moved her ass on up there to Vancouver as soon as he asked, typical Maggie fashion. I told her not to, warned her about getting serious, but she didn't listen. She never does.

I guess it's not all that bad. The guy is half decent. A little short but okay. Has a steady job at a bank and everything so they're all right for money. I guess I'm happy. Yeah, I'm happy for her. In some ways, I am definitely happy for her.

We still keep in touch. We talk on the phone sometimes, but the long distance is expensive for her, and I'm not good on the phone. So we usually stick to e-mails.

She's pregnant. Found out last week. I couldn't believe it. I was the first person she told, after her guy, of course. She is really just out of her damn mind.

Pregnant at her age! But she was so damn happy, I could tell in the e-mail. So I didn't tell her how crazy she was. I just keep thinking, Christ, Maggie and her own little baby.

It's due at the end of the year, so I figure I'll make a trip up there to meet the little thing. Maybe stick around for Christmas. She said that I can be the baby's granddaddy. I don't want to be, particularly, but it was nice of her to offer.

I know it's crazy of me, but I keep thinking I see her walking into the bar. I'll see someone with red hair out of the corner of my eye, and I'll think it's Maggie, come to surprise me, that she's back to visit. But it's never been her. I just go back to my book and my beer, and try to enjoy the quiet. A part of me thinks that maybe one day she will surprise me. It'd be a real Maggie thing to do.

So, yeah, some nights, I do get to missing her.

Some nights.

Sweetieface

Sam sits alone in the bar. Grace is twenty minutes late.

Looking out into the frosty dark, Sam sees John, a guy he used to play pickup baseball with. As he raises his arm to wave, he realizes it's not John, just a guy who looks almost the same. Why does everyone look the same here?

Earlier that evening, he went for dinner with his stepfather. It was their tradition to eat the first meal alone when he came home from school, "just the men." In the middle of their burgers, his stepfather said, "In your life, people are going to give you every opportunity to be weak. All they'll ever want is for you to be strong." He looked strange, childlike when he told Sam this. Now, the words swirl around Sam's mouth, like a piece of gum he doesn't know where to spit.

Drinking quickly, he feels the alcohol in his head.

Then, he sees her. Tall, dark, with an angled face. He feels his face transform for a short second and switches it back, not wanting her to know her effect but sure she sees the difference.

He stands to meet her.

"Shit, Sam! I'm so sorry. I got caught up at home. I totally lost track of time. Have you been waiting forever?"

Sam lies, without thinking.

"No! No, I've been here for, like, a minute, don't worry about it."

"I'm so sorry. I just get so crazy before I'm leaving the house. I can't remember a thing I need, and then I look at the clock—"

"Grace?"

"Yeah?"

"Shut the fuck up."

Grace finds Sam's eyes and laughs, very truthful. She feels suddenly comfortable, at home for the first time in a while.

The history of Grace and Sam settles between them, tangible. She wants to touch it, so she holds his shoulder.

"It's so good to see you," she says, finally breathing.

"Yeah, you look great," he says, still smiling.

"Really? I don't look fatter?"

"Are you actually going to ask me that every time I see you for the rest of your life?"

Grace stares at Sam for a moment.

"Probably."

Grace knows she doesn't look the same as she did the last time she saw Sam, eight months ago. With the weight, her face looks wholly different, bearing almost no resemblance to who she used to be. Now that she's thinking about it, she can't remember being who she used to be. There has been so much alcohol, so many lonely invaders between the two.

Sam is still smiling at her. She hugs him, tightly, and for a long moment.

"I missed you, Sam," she says.

Grace is casual when she says things like "I missed you" or "I love you," and Sam knows that about her. He's not casual like that, but her absence in his life was palpable. He missed her, so much, and in a way that hits him only now that they are together again. She lets go before he does.

Grace takes off her coat and sits down. Sam likes her dress, looking at it so discreetly she can't notice.

"Oh my God, it's exactly the same in here," she says.

"I know, eh?"

"Coming home, I feel like nothing ever changes."

"Yeah. I don't know. I like that about coming home, though. I like that it's always the same."

She smiles at him.

"Oh my God, Sam! Do you remember that time when we came in here and Graham and I had just broken up, and I was so depressed and you wanted to cheer me up, and we did shot for shot, and I beat you? And it was, like, a Wednesday in Grade 11?"

"You didn't beat me! I quit!"

"Liar!"

"You're a liar! I carried your ass home that night. If you passed out, that means I won."

"Oh, fine, by default."

Sam remembers that Grace invited him in, drunk, heartbroken, and he could have had her if he wanted. But he didn't want it to be like that. He put her to bed, and without touching her, even though he could have, he left. He knows she does not remember that night. Not how he does, anyway.

"Sam, do you have to go to the bar to order?" she asks.

"Yeah, I think . . ."

She won't go to the bar to order. He wonders why she bothers asking him questions that she doesn't want answered.

She lifts her arm and waves it at the waitress. "Hi! Hi! Over here!"

"What can I get you?"

"Oh, uhm . . . Sam, what are you drinking?"

"Just beer."

Grace looks up and around the bar, clicking her tongue, just so everyone knows she's thinking.

"I'll have a double vodka and soda?"

"Any type of vodka?" asks the waitress.

"The cheapest," she says and smiles.

"Wow, that big city has made you so sophisticated." Sam's never forgiven that she moved to Chicago to study philosophy and literature. He knows the move was motivated by a sense that she was close to some discovery about herself. It hasn't come.

"Fuck you. How are you? What's new? Tell me stuff!"

"I'm good. Things are, you know, the same really. School's going good—"

"I don't understand how you can do science in university. Isn't it, like, so hard?"

"Yeah, kind of. It's easy for me, though, so I like it. And Guelph is good, you know, it's Guelph, but the boys are good."

"Really? How are they? How's Booty?"

Booty has been Sam's best friend forever. No one quite knows why he is called Booty, has been since middle school, and there's no changing it now.

"Failing. Drunk a lot. The same."

"That warms my heart. And how's Lily?"

Hearing her name, Sam freezes.

"She's good, we're good. We're, um . . . talking about maybe going to Europe this summer."

"Really?" Grace smiles, trying to look happy. "So you and Lily are totally in love, huh?"

"Ah, well, I don't know. We don't really talk about that stuff, so . . ."

"But you love her."

Sam might love Lily. He thinks. Sometimes.

"Yeah, I mean we've been together for . . . ever, so . . ."

Before Sam has to continue, the waitress brings Grace her drink. Sam's relieved. He hates talking about Lily with Grace. As the waitress walks away, he notices that she's not half bad. If Grace wasn't with him, he'd take a longer look.

Grace grabs her drink in both hands, moving it from the table to her lips without pause.

"Oh, thank God, I've had such a day," she says.

"What happened?"

"Oh, nothing really. Luke and I have just been fighting lately. He's driving me fucking nuts."

Sam tries his hardest to act concerned. He knows they'd gotten serious quickly, as is often the case with Grace. She possesses an uncanny ability to commit to those who don't want to commit to her, never fully understanding that it isn't meant to be a one-sided bargain.

"What's going on?"

"It's just, like . . . I don't know, we're really different. He's so, he's one of those people who seems really interesting at first, because he's in a band and everything. I thought we had so much in common, and on the surface, we do but it's not the stuff that matters. Like, I don't think he understands me. Not really. I don't know. You met him that one time when you came to visit me. At his show, right? What'd you think?"

Sam thought he was a fucking idiot.

"He was cool."

"Yeah, he is cool," says Grace.

"Do you like his band?" Sam asks.

"Honestly?"

"Yes, honestly. Between us."

"I hate them!"

They laugh so loudly that the couple next to them stares. Grace notices and starts laughing louder. They grin at each other like children who've agreed on something forbidden.

"But maybe I hate them because I'm not, like, really cool, in the way he's really cool. Maybe it's too advanced for me or something," says Grace.

"You do like Coldplay."

"Well, I did. I can't listen to them anymore."

"Why?"

Grace looks down at her drink. She looks up at Sam again and smiles, but her lips, full and red, look stretched and uneven.

"I don't want to tell you," she says.

"Why?"

"Because you'll make fun of me."

Sam knows immediately, instinctively, where this conversation is going, and he doesn't like it.

"Oh no. Not because of—"

"Yes. Because of Graham. Because we listened to them together, because we liked them . . . together."

"Okay, that just proves that I'm right. That guy was a douche."

"Yeah, well, I don't know."

"How is he not?" Sam asks her. He knows he's right and Grace does too, but she can't quite bring herself to really know it, in a lasting way. That it's that black and white; that he was all bad, no good, but she had always held her breath for too a hair long. Blind and suffocating, she could never call anything.

"Well, he loved me, Sam. Like he really loved me. Luke is the douche—he doesn't really love me, not at all. That's why we fight, even though he's home with me for Christmas. He can't even begin to touch the part of me that Graham touched. He doesn't even want to try. And it's embarrassing, but it makes me miss Graham. So there you are. I still miss Graham."

"Graham didn't really love you."

"What do you mean?"

"He cheated on you, all those times."

"It must look so simple from the outside," says Grace.

"Sam, he was fucked up, he fucked up, but that doesn't have anything to do with how much you love people. I know he really loved me."

"No, Grace, someone who really loved you wouldn't be able to do that to you."

"I don't know. I thought it was that cut and dried when we broke up. I'm not sure now."

Then Sam sees the sadness in her face again and thinks that maybe he's gone too far.

"You know what's fucked? I'd want Luke to cheat on me, if it meant he would look at me how Graham did, even once. I just want to know that someone else will look at me like that. But I tell myself that people love differently and that Luke does love me. I tell myself that it's not always obvious when people really love you. Maybe it can be under the surface."

That's true, thinks Sam. You can keep it hidden. But it hurts.

"Jesus Christ, all this shit is just depressing," she says.

The privacy of that kind of love scars.

"Yeah." He doesn't know why he's laughing.

"Question," she says.

"Shoot," he says.

"Does Lily make you more happy or unhappy?"

He's thrown off kilter. "Happy! Definitely more happy."

"Really?"

"Yeah, she's really smart, and funny, and, well, you know her."

Grace thinks for a moment.

"I don't know her. She doesn't talk."

Sam met Lily at the beginning of university and has always tried very hard to keep her and Grace apart. Lily is the kind of girl who doesn't follow politics. She can't remember the last time she fought with someone. She is studying to be a gym teacher and tries every day to wear one blue item of clothing. Her hair is always remarkably the same, somehow untouched and unmoved from the moment she wakes up in the morning. It took Sam two years to realize that she didn't wear any makeup at all.

She told Sam once that she hated the absence of him more than she loved the presence of him and thought that was the mark of a good relationship.

"Well, yeah, it's hard to know Lily. To really know her, but it's good between us. I can't complain, right? It's easy. And, it's been so long that sometimes I feel like if we broke up it'd be like losing an arm or something."

Grace takes her drink, spilling some on her dress and the table, not noticing.

"Yeah! Yeah, that's kind of how it feels. I mean, breaking up, it's . . . it's a fucked-up concept in general, especially if you've been with someone for a long time. Think about it. One day, you have this conversation with someone who you've spent so much time with, and who you've been so intimate with, and the conversation can be one-sided, and you say, like, one sentence, like: 'I want to break up,' and then however you acted before, whatever you were before, it's suddenly not allowed. Gone. That's bullshit! You can't erase everything that you feel for someone in one conversation. And for so long after that, the person is still so active in your mind, you know?"

"But some people break up for years."

"That's my point. I think breaking up, in a real sense, takes a really long time. Like it takes months not to associate everything about relationships with that one person. I mean, I'm with Luke, at least for the time being, right? But I think I'm still breaking up with Graham. Everyday I'm a little further away from who I was with him, but it's not completely gone. It might never be. Don't you think breaking up is a fucked concept?"

"Yeah, but I don't know because Lily is my first real girlfriend, so I've never been through heartbreak before."

"Maybe you won't have to. Maybe you guys won't ever break up."

Grace is trying to be kind to Sam, but the thought of being with Lily forever makes him feel violently sick.

"Well, sometimes I wonder what it would be like to be single. Or just not with her. Sometimes I get curious for what something else would be like."

"Yeah. It must be hard to be faithful, hey?"

Looking at Grace, it is hard.

"Sometimes it's hard. It's not hard at school because we're together so much, like she's in front of me all the time. It's not that I see new girls all the time that I want to fuck, but it's the knowing that I can't, couldn't. That's hard."

She's drinking heavily.

"Only sometimes," he adds.

"Do you like fucking her?"

Grace has an adopted bravado about sex. She talks about it

roughly, as if that makes all her mistakes, all the hurt, matter less.

"Yeah. Yeah, it's good."

"Good like great or good like good?"

He's not sure how to answer. Lily is the only girl he's ever been with, but Grace doesn't know that.

One night, not long ago, he pretended it was Grace he was making love to, but it was like Lily knew. He could have sworn her face became Grace's face. Her movements became Grace's movements. She was dominant, angry; an animal. She wrapped her hands around his neck. She let him pour everything inside into her.

When he came, she turned into Lily again.

"Good like, I don't know. Good like great."

"Fuck you! I am so jealous!"

"It's not great with Luke?"

She looks at him like she's at a loss, as if she doesn't know what to make of anything, as if it's just her body present, as if it's not her Luke's inside of.

"It's sophisticated. Like we go and do stuff in the city and everything. We don't just fuck all the time, so there's a build-up. But it's really shitty sometimes. Most times."

"Really? What's shitty about it?"

Sam doesn't know why he's asking. He doesn't want to know more.

"I don't feel like he really wants me. I think if I knew he really wanted me I could loosen up. And it's me too; I'm awkward with him. I know I was better with Graham. It's strange. We don't fuck and we don't make love. We just have sex."

"I'm sure he wants you, Grace," says Sam without thinking. I'm drunk, he thinks. Sober Sam would have never said that so casually.

"No, I think I'm too available to him, and it's unattractive."

Grace pushes her glass away.

"How?"

"I just come running every time he calls. And we're always fighting and he's an asshole to me, but if he wants me to come over, I go. I don't even think that I really love him, but I stick around."

"Well, why do you think you do it?"

Looking at her face, he has nowhere to hide.

"I don't know. Isn't that sad?"

"It is sad," he says finally.

Grace opens her mouth to say something as Sam leans forward, but the waitress comes by again. Sam wants her to go away so he can hear what Grace will say next.

"Can I get you another round?" asks the waitress.

Grace says yes because even when she tries to drown her sorrows, they learn how to swim.

"Sam, order something real," she says.

"Okay, shots?"

"Yes! Bring us four tequila, and I'll have the same again."

"Okay, I'll have a double rum and Coke," he says.

"Finally!" says Grace. "What were we talking about?"

"Did you forget already, drunky?"

"Yeah, kind of."

Sam remembers what Grace was talking about.

"I don't really remember either," he says.

"Do you ever wonder why we even bother? Why do we try to figure this shit out? Relationships, men, it doesn't make me happy."

"It must, somewhere."

"Maybe at the beginning. That feeling you get at the beginning."

"That feeling's bullshit."

"What?"

"It's not real."

"Do you ever think that maybe nothing is really real? That it's all just in our heads?"

"Maybe. What do you want?" he asks her.

Grace looks away for a second. The bar has become darker, and he has to strain to see her.

"To be with someone I love. Who loves me too. Honestly. That's it."

"No, you don't."

If that's what you wanted, we'd be together, he thinks.

But it is way more complicated than that.

The waitress puts the shots on the table. Grace takes two and leaves two for Sam.

"To misery."

"Eat your heart out."

They take the shots, quickly, one after the other. The tequila's cheap. It burns.

"Wow," says Grace.

"Sweet Jesus."

"I feel a little drunk," says Grace, pleased.

"Good."

Everything around them is unfocused.

"So you don't think that feeling exists? Like that feeling that makes everything else not matter? The feeling you get loving someone?" she asks.

Words fall through Sam. For years, he's gone back and forth, telling himself his feelings are not real, telling himself she's not who he thinks she is, telling himself to let it go and be happy without her.

"For sure it exists because people feel it all the time. I just don't know if that feeling is grounds for a relationship. It's not realistic."

"Huh."

"I don't know if it's anything other than what you want to feel about that person. And when you build someone up so much, they can't be real to you. So I think it's bullshit. Because usually that person doesn't feel the same way about you, or is so different in reality that it's like two different people you are dealing with. I mean, arranged marriages are more successful than regular ones. Just think about that. Just think about that for one second. Clearly, a relationship needs a lot more than love to work."

After Sam's said that, he feels safe again, but when he looks down at his hands, they're trembling. He rests them on his knees under the table, and when he looks away from them and up again, Grace is staring at him.

"That's fucked, Sam. If you aren't grounding a relationship on love, then why do it at all? Maybe people are not meant for relationships or monogamy. My parents aren't happy, your parents aren't happy. What the fuck is everyone doing?"

"Settling? Probably settling?"

Silence settles between them, but no one in the bar seems to notice. Strangers speak louder than before.

Then Sam looks at Grace, exactly the way she wants to be looked at, but she can't see it.

"Oh my God, there's this fucking lunatic in Chicago, near my building, and every day he would call out to me, 'Sweetieface! Sweetieface! You're such a sweetieface!' Usually, I'd ignore him, or wave, or give him the finger, but finally I was like No, this guy talks to me every day. He looks harmless, right? So I go up to him, and I say, 'Hi! I'm Grace,' and he says, 'Hi, I'm Mark or Dave' or something, I can't remember his name."

Sam knows this is a story she's wanted to tell for weeks. It's rehearsed. She saves stories like this. She doesn't want to tell them to the wrong person, looking stupid or crazy, so she's waited, until she's drunk with someone who doesn't scare her.

For someone who is so interesting without effort, he's never met anybody more terrified of being plain.

"And it's fucking freezing out, right? This is, like, two weeks ago, so I ask him if I can buy him a coffee and then we start talking a little, and he says to me, 'Sweetieface, there are two types of people in this world. There are people who play it real safe and never go for what they want, they might not even know what they really want. Then there are the people who know what they want, who feel it burning so much inside them, so that they have no choice but to just go out and get it.' Then he goes, 'Usually, they don't get it, but they try. So there are people who try and there are people who don't try. The people who don't try, they look like they win because they don't obviously lose. But the people who try and lose, they win. Because they're brave.' And it really made me think, you know? Maybe it's not men and women. Maybe it's brave and not brave."

"Yeah. Which one are you?"

For a moment everything is stripped from her face.

"I feel like I'm brave, but I don't know. I'm scared shitless a lot of the time. What are you?"

He's not brave, and he knows it.

"I want to be brave."

Sam allows himself, for the briefest of moments, to touch her hand. He holds it gently at first, then tighter.

"I'm hammered," she says. "Let's smoke."

"You don't smoke," he says, not looking away.

"I smoke when I'm drunk. Come on, Dad, let's smoke."

Grace and Sam stand outside. It's cold, and the street is buzzing with the feeling that exists only at Christmastime. It's the hope that change is around the corner, good change, underscored by the nostalgia of all that hasn't changed, all that will never change. Colourful Christmas lights shine on a tree above them. Tinny sounds of a radio carol float from some joint across the street.

It's good to be home, thinks Sam.

Grace takes her first real drag, and then can't breathe.

"I told you, you don't smoke!" Sam says, laughing.

"Fine, but it's still fun," she says, coughing.

Grace leans on Sam, unable to keep her balance. Sam thinks it's the fresh air, or the cigarettes, or both, that's made everything go to her head.

"Sa-a-am, I'm cold," she slurs.

Grace goes to sit on the curb, but Sam stops her, pulling her up gently, under her arms.

"You're ridiculous," he says.

She takes a deep breath. "I think icicles are growing inside me," she says.

"Take my coat."

"But then you'll be cold."

"Not for long, I'm almost done," says Sam, holding his cigarette to show her.

He takes off his big brown coat and places it on her shoulders gently. He doesn't want to hurt her. For some reason, he tells him-self to be careful.

"Oh my God, thank you."

Grace shivers. Sam puts his arm around her, to keep her warmer. He looks down at her, drowning in his coat.

"Better?" he asks.

"Yes, better. Your arm feels nice," she whispers.

"Thanks."

He never wants to move it.

"Sam?"

"Yes?"

"Do you think I'm brave?"

"Yes."

"Good. I think you're brave too."

"I want to be brave," he says again.

They stand, so close together, for a few moments. Grace isn't really present, but for Sam only this moment exists. He knows it will end soon.

He puts his cigarette out.

"C'mon, it's fucking cold. Let's go in," he says.

"I think we should take more shots," says Grace.

"Are you sure?"

"Of course I'm sure, you puss." She doesn't need another drink. He knows he should stop her, but he doesn't want to.

"Two tequila," says Sam.

"Four! I'll buy," she says, leaning over the bar.

"Okay, four," he says, looking at her softness. He lets himself look for longer than he would usually.

"I think I should break up with Luke."

"Yeah?" he says, not letting anything float to the surface.

"Yeah, I hate him."

The bartender slams the shots in front of them. Grace takes a twenty out of her bra and puts it on the bar.

"If you hate him, then you should," says Sam.

Grace slides two shots in front of Sam, takes the other two. She brings one up near her face, making a toast.

"To breakups."

"Cheers."

They take the shots, in rapid succession, without breathing, without blinking.

"Motherfucker," says Grace.

Grace winces. This surprises Sam. She never lets herself wince when people are watching.

"Now who's a tough guy, huh?" he asks.

Sam doesn't wince. The shots don't even burn going down. They taste like water.

"Sam! I love this song!"

"Me too."

"Let's dance, Sam!"

"I don't dance."

"Oh, come on, it's me, and you're drunk, and nobody's here."

Sam looks around the bar. It's empty. When did everyone leave?

"Please, Sam? I love this song."

When she's standing there she looks so beautiful. Her hair has fallen, and she looks drunk, and happy, and finally relaxed enough to be herself. Sam is overcome with a furious desire to touch her, to hold her, to be against her. He wishes he could tell her how he feels. But words don't ever fit how he feels for her. He thinks then that maybe some things are meant only to be felt, forever unspoken and misunderstood, lonesome and unfair.

Then he looks at her again. He can't stop himself.

He grabs her and pulls her close. She falls into him. Her hands find his shoulders, and he holds her waist. They move with an intimacy usually saved for when they are alone. Grace rests her head on Sam.

He thinks a new Sam is born when he holds her. The brave Sam. The Sam he wants to be. The man who doesn't breathe in him alone. They continue to sway, now cheek to cheek.

She feels so soft.

When the song ends, Sam doesn't let go of her. They stay, folded together, standing in the bar.

She speaks.

"Sam, I think I need to sit down. Can we sit down?"

"Yeah, let's sit down," he says.

Grace is unsteady on her feet. Her dress has slid off her shoulder. She pulls it up. She touches her face.

"I look crazy. I'm going to the washroom."

"You don't look crazy," says Sam.

"Stop lying."

Sam smiles at her, and he's certain she can feel him watching her walk away.

Sam sits slumped on his chair waiting for Grace. He can't feel his legs beneath him.

He's going to tell her.

Be brave, Sam.

Forget Lily, forget everything, forget everyone.

Be brave, Sam.

Tell her. Go on, love her.

Love her forever.

Grace comes back to the table. She sits down. She looks like she's been crying.

Be brave, Sam.

"Grace, I . . ."

"Sam, I have to go."

"What?"

"Yeah, I'm just really fucked, and Luke just texted me back and apologized and I just have to go see him. I'm going to just take a cab home. I'm just really fucked. I need to go to bed. I'm really fucked. I don't feel well."

She gets up, and so does he, but the sound is sucked out of the room.

"Sam, tonight was really fun," says Grace, but she sounds like she's under water.

"Yeah, it was really fun," he can feel himself say, but he's surprised when it comes out of his mouth.

It echoes.

"It was really good to see you, I really missed you," she says.

"You too."

All he can hear is his own voice in his head. Be brave, Sam.

"I have to go, I'm so fucked, I'll call you tomorrow," she says.

"Do you need me to walk you out?"

"Nah," she says as she throws her coat on, graceless and unco-ordinated.

She hugs him, and kisses him on the cheek.

"Bye, Grace."

"Bye, Sam."

And Grace leaves Sam just how she found him; alone at a table with half a drink.

Be brave, Sam, he says to himself once more.

All he can hear is his heart beating; the noise he sat there making, not daring to move, not even when the room goes dark.

Forever Ago

There isn't a day that goes by when I don't think of you.

When Amy smiles at me, the morning light hitting her face, having left some in shadow, I see you lying next to me. There is something about her expression, the sadness under her skin. You both share a vulnerability brought on by sleep.

Amy, that's my girlfriend.

I see you when I'm not looking, when I don't expect to see you at all. A woman passes me on the street with hair like yours. Is your hair different now? A friend at work talks how you do. I eat lunch with her, ask her questions I want to ask you. Amy falls asleep in my arms when I'm drunk and I drift into the arms of elsewhere.

Elsewhere holds me.

With all the time, you've become two-dimensional. You are like a photograph, not close enough to touch, bent and worn. Pictures are criminal. No one ever looks like themselves because no one even wants to, but still these images of you tunnel into me and stick like the cavities in my teeth.

Why can life only be understood?

We were twenty. We walked through the concrete, suffocating streets of the city and you wore a flowered scarf. You'd got it from your grandmother. Pink with red flowers. I thought it was ugly and I told you. You wore it because you loved her smell.

I know she's dead because I saw the obituary you posted on

Facebook. I wrote you to tell you how sorry I was. You never wrote back. You didn't have to, but I felt so bad about what I'd said about the scarf.

I wonder now if you searched in vain for my obituary, curious if I was dead or alive, if you ever needed proof that I existed once and no longer.

I keep seeing that scarf. It won't leave me alone.

In the park, you told me you were sad. I asked why. You said the worst loss was the kind you could feel happening.

I didn't know you were talking about us.

I have become a person I never thought I'd be.

It was summer turning into fall and it got dark earlier than we expected. We sat on your wood floor, no furniture, no bed, no money, nothing at all, and even though you were sad, we laughed until we cried.

Do you remember any of that?

Did I make that up?

Were we happy?

I forget how your voice sounds. The hours we spent talking— and I can't remember your voice.

Do you sometimes think that if we'd taken a left instead of a right, if we'd stayed home instead of going to the bar, if we'd seen that movie, if one small thing was different, we'd still be together? If we'd met later, if we'd met earlier, if we'd never met at all?

Why can life only be understood backwards?

I tell Amy I love her. It's not how I loved you. I can't decide if that means I don't love her at all. No one's like you, but with a touch, a gesture, a sound, you're right here, all over me again. I wonder if it's in the way they make me feel. If all those feelings began and ended in you, trickling away like water down a drain.

Is the man you're with like me?

Why didn't I just try? Why didn't I stick it out? Why didn't I listen to you?

I'm writing this too quickly.

I thought I saw you about a year ago. It was Christmastime, and your hair was shorter. The woman I thought was you was carrying a briefcase. But you got lost in the rush hour crowd of the New York City subway. Since then, I've wondered if I'll ever see you again. Sometimes I get off at that stop for no reason other than that you might be there. What would we talk about? How would I speak to you? What would I say?

"Do you really carry a briefcase?"

Do you remember when we made love for the last time? You asked me not to look as you got dressed. You said I didn't have to ask you the same because you couldn't see through your tears. I asked if we shouldn't have and you just shrugged and asked, "What else were we going to do?"

You hated me and I knew it. The war had begun and ended, and we walked around each other like refugees or burn victims; armless, only half a head of hair with ugly, graphed skin.

I got that letter you sent me a year later. I should have replied. I didn't because I had just gotten your hairs off my fucking pillowcase.

Do you remember those nights when we would watch three movies in a row? You started smoking weed with me because you couldn't sleep. Do you still have insomnia?

Do you still only order poached eggs and bacon at restaurants?

Do you remember when your dad told you he felt no emotions? Only anger and never sadness? He said the world offended him and no other thing? And I told you that anger was a useful emotion and that obviously anger is just how he relates to everything. You looked at me, disgusted. "That's not the point." And then later, you told me, "My father feels profound sadness all the time and that's why he said that. That's the only reason anyone could say something like that."

You asked why I couldn't be more of a human being, and I tried to argue with you about the existence of aliens.

I knew then that your father was your child. I realized that I'd missed the point too late, but I did realize. What does that count for?

I have these notions about you. You live quietly but happily. You have a child. Getting dressed and you wonder if I'd like what you are wearing. Your kid cries in the other room. You make him breakfast. You dance in the dark.

Have you gotten what you wanted?

You are not just a physical being anymore: skin, bones, blood. You are composed of thoughts, ideas, feelings; all that I gave away long ago. You are a myriad of things that probably have nothing to do with you. I hate you for it.

I know it's my fault that so much time has fallen between us. I didn't want it this way.

Is time passing this fucking fast for you too?

I'm sorry for writing you. I'm sorry I'm asking you so many questions.

There's just one last thing I want to know.

Do you think of me?

The Falling Action

"'Bout ye?"

I remember those words because I'll never forget them, not in one million years.

It was September 1971. I was sittin' in a pub, this real shite-hole in Belfast. I don't know why I keep having to say *in Belfast*, not like I ever left the place. It was my first time there because our usual was closed. It was well into the night and I wanted a final pint, but I couldn't get the attention of the waitress. Your woman was too busy slabbering with some wee bastard, but I was busting for one, like. So I went up to the bar and ordered it myself.

And there she was. Kate. My beautiful Kate.

If ye had told me right then and there that this woulda been the girl to change my life, I woulda believed ya. People are always sayin', No way would I'da known if someone told me before. But I woulda believed you immediately. Pretty much everything in this story I woulda believed if you'd told it all out to me before like I'm here telling you.

Standing at that bar, she looked like nobody I ever seen before. She did not look like a regular Belfast bird, no way. She had this real natural gorgeousness to her and, no offence, but the birds aren't like that here.

She had this white skin, skin that was so pale you could almost see the blue of her veins under it. It was real delicate, but she had this happy glow to her, and so her skin shone a nice pink in her cheeks. And she had this short hairstyle. Her hair was jet black, and against her white skin she looked like some wood angel mixed with Snow White. Really special.

But the most prettiest part of her was her eyes. No question, like. Her eyes were unreal, so they were. They were violet. Never in my life had I ever seen someone with violet eyes before. I mean, fuck me!

Actually, she said, "'Bout ye?" twice because I was stuck staring at her for so long.

"'Bout ye?"

"Aye, Guinness?" I said that with this real faggot voice. I was so stunned and nervous talking to her that I lost my own voice for a minute. Luckily, I recovered fast. I like to pride myself on recoverin' fast.

"Got ya."

"You been working here long?" I'm a proper faggot. Who asks somethin' like that?

"Nah, just a few weeks, like. You come here a lot?" she asked, turning around, smiling.

"Now and again. What're ya called, darlin'?"

"Kate." Then she smiled again. Kate. That was the most perfect name.

"I'm Sean."

"Ah, right then. Well, here's your Guinness."

I knew the conversation might be done just then if I left with my Guinness and went back to my dumb mates, so I needed to find a way to keep talking to her. I had to get to know her, or at least smell her hair or somethin', anythin'. Really, I woulda been chuffed with anythin'.

"I'm gonna sit here for a bit and keep yourself company. My mates are talking about the match and I can't stand it a second longer," I told her.

"You don't like football?"

"Now and again, but it's not my favourite topic, like." And then I probably smiled at her like a ball bag. I was lying through my teeth too. I love football and I love talking about it, probably more than all else. But I wanted to impress her so I acted different than I really was.

"Not your typical man then, are ya?"

She smiled at me. I think she seen me for the first ever time then. She really took notice of me then, so she did.

"I'm the same. I think there's no point in being like anybody else."

She was telling the truth there. She was not like anybody else. She was honest and beautiful and smart and way too good for me. Sad part was that I was more like everyone else than she knew, even than I really knew. Maybe things woulda been okay if I was my own man.

"So what are you like then, Kate?"

She laughed. She had this real perfect laugh. Big, and it vibrated through any space around her. She truly loved laughing, like.

"Sicka working here, I'll tell you."

"Why's that?"

"Sicka Belfast, really. I want to travel, but I'm skint so I'm working here for the time bein'. How 'bout yourself? What's the craic with you, like?"

"Da's a coalminer. I work with him."

"How old are ye? You look 'bout my age."

"Twenty-three. Yourself?"

"Just about to turn twenty-one. You got a young face."

"I'll take that as a compliment."

Then she smiled again.

I felt elated. This gorgeous bird was complimenting me, the woman of my dreams thought I was not half bad. I was over the moon! Over the bloody moon!

I heard my mate Couch calling me. He always had horrible timing, God rest his soul.

"C'mon, faggot! This waitress is shite."

My mates all had their jackets on, and they were all well pissed. It was pretty much my time to exit unless I wanted Kate to think I kept company with dozy fucken' muppets, which was the God's honest, but I didn't want her knowin' that, like.

When I turned back to her she was laughing her beautiful laugh, but I could tell she was a little disappointed the conversation was over. Picture how your man felt! I was gutted! I had to leave this perfect angel for my ball-bag, wanker, faggot, muppet mates.

"Well, looks like you've gotta go," she said to me.

But I knew I couldn't be a dozy cunt myself.

"Listen, would ye have dinner with me?"

She gave me her number. She had real nice handwriting too. Like a princess or something would.

"Don't go being like all those other lads and not calling me for a few days, leavin' me high and dry waiting by the phone. Call me tomorrow. And if ye don't call me, I'll cut yer wee balls off with a rusty knife the next time I see ye in this bar."

Then she winked at me.

And right then, I knew it. I loved her.

A lot of things have changed since then. Not like I don't love her anymore, that's not changed. That's not ever gonna change, not for me. But it was a real dirty time in Belfast then, "The Troubles."

I always thought calling it "The Troubles" was a kind of laugh, like. We were trying to sugarcoat how fucking horrible it was then, so we were. Oh, just "The Troubles." No. The "fucken'-cunt-shits" would be more like it. Or the "fucken' worst time in the history of Belfast" would be even more like it. Or "literal fucken'-cunt-shits Hell on Earth" would be even more-more like it.

But things are well different there now. At least they are from where I'm lookin' at it. I mean, we've got a fucken' opera house there now. Why the people of Belfast would wanna listen to someone else's tragedies is well beyond me, but that's what I'm sayin' to ye.

It ain't so tragic now. "The Troubles" are done now. There are Catholic areas, Hun areas still. There is still some distance separating us, ya know what I mean. Since the talks things have settled down but not ended. Never ended. But look, I mean, the Reverend Ian Paisley, that spectacular arsehole, he even said that we were on the way to peace, and all that blah, blah, blah.

And from up here, I got to be honest, he has a point. It looks better. I mean, me wee sister couldn't even go into downtown Belfast around the time I met Kate, and now, you got young girls running all over, not a care in the world. The luxury, like. We didn't have parks. We didn't have a post office.

It seems crazy now, it all seems so fucken' crazy now, but my actions, the actions of every involved man, they made sense in context.

I was fifteen when I joined the IRA. I was just a wee boy, but in my mind, I was a man. We all thought we were men then. The people that recruited us, they knew that and they took advantage of that.

Ah, nah, fuck what I just said. We weren't recruited, not really. I wanted to be a part of it. I wanted to fight for my people. I wanted to help the Catholics, and I wanted everyone who said, "For God and Ulster" to eat shit and die because they didn't have no business with God. That's how ye feel after ya seen yer big brother die at the hands of them. Truth is, my big brother died all over me.

So ya got to remember what it was like in 1971. There were people, my people, being killed every godforsaken day, for as long as I could remember, and that was before my brother, James. When I met Kate, they were lockin' us up for no reason other than they could, arrest without trial, Bloody Sunday was yet to come, and things were getting worse and were about to keep getting worse for Catholics. We were getting fucked up the arse, hard, left, right, centre. James had died for nothing because nothing was changing. Petrol bombs under cars, firebombs in homes, shootings, rubber bullets, real bullets, 3:00 AM searches, hurtin' babies and raping women, beatings, killings, death. My people. Dead everywhere I looked.

Just imagine how that feels. Nah, you can't. If it ain't happened to you, you can't, and I shouldn't have asked you to because you can't.

But if James hadn't been shot three times in his head by useless fucken' cunt Hun thugs for no reason other than bein' Catholic, I don't think I woulda been involved. I know I wouldnta been. But after somethin' like that happens to you, after you see yer ma with that kind of pain, you see yer da turn away from God, after you see yer big brother in a coffin, well, a lot of your brain, a lot of the part that thinks, it shuts right down. Yer guts are sucked right outta ya and replaced by this angry, violent feelin', this feelin' like nothing matters except gettin' them back. Except tryin' to change things. Except doin' to them what they done to you. Thus buryin' that sufferin' in yerself.

As far as I was concerned, hearts only beat in Catholics. God only spoke to Catholics. Only Catholic mas cried. It was us versus them. So killing a Prod? Some poor Prod fuck losing his big brother at my hands? Thinking about a Prod as a person? It doesn't even enter your fucken' head.

When I signed up I was proud. I was proud that I was a soldier for my side. And I think if I had it to do all again, I probably woulda. I don't see how I couldn't have.

Unless I knew about Kate. If I had known about Kate beforehand, nah. No fucken' way. Even if they had still took James, no fucken' way, I never woulda.

Because ya know that part of you I said that shuts down forever? The thinking part? Well, I felt that comin' back with Kate. I felt that comin' back a little durin' the short time we got ta spend together. It scared me shiteless, like, but it came back wit' her.

So, yeah, had I known about her, nah, I woulda avoided it much as I could.

But this is a love story.

I called her up the very next day. And not jus' because she told me too, I was dyin' to, like. I had to do everythin' in my power to not call her again and again and again all night 'til she picked up. I waited 'til probably half noon that day and I rang her. I'd be lyin' to ye if I said I wasn't a bit pissed, but in my opinion, there's nothing wrong with a few for good luck.

When she picked up, my heart skipped near eighty-three beats.

"Hullo?" She sounded even lovelier on the phone than I had remembered.

"Ye, hullo. Alrigh', Kate? It's Sean."

"Oh, Sean. Ye called. Good thing fer you. I was just sharpenin' me knife here."

That's one thing I really loved about her, she was mad and I loved it, all of it. Because all people are mad and it takes a real brave one to be mad and honest 'bout it.

"Wha?"

"I'm only foolin' with ye! What's the craic?"

"Nuttin, like. What's the craic with ye?"

"Juss getting ready for work."

"When are ye done tonight?"

"Around nine, I'm leaving early actually, me mate is playin' a show. It's just a wee small set."

"Oh, nice one."

"You wanna come with me?"

I remember thinking then that this was not how I had planned things. I was supposed to be asking her, not the other way 'round. But I'm not such a dozy cunt that I didn't see a good openin' and take it. I really admired that she had more balls than me.

"Yeah, I'd love to, like. I'll pick you up when yer done?"

"Say 8:45. I got to put me face on before seein' ya."

"Yer face is perfect just how it is."

I could hear her go silent on the other side of the conversation. I know this is a crazy thing to say, but I could feel her smiling all the way through the phone.

"Okay, well . . . see ya tonight."

"I can'y wait. Bye, now."

"Bye, Sean."

I waited until she hung up before I hung up the phone. And when I did, I could feel meself gettin' the nervous sweats. It was only seven hours 'til I saw her, and this date had to go perfectly or else I'd be cursin' myself forever, like.

Ever since I'd met her I felt the feelin' in my stomach that I used to get as a wee boy before anything bad had happened. When I was running down a hill at full speed that was too steep for me and I knew I would fall flat on me arse, and fall hard, any second, but I was laughing the whole way down.

When I picked her up outside the bar after work, she looked even better than I remembered. She had on this lovely red dress and it matched the red in her cheeks. She wasn't wearin' no makeup, but believe me, she didn't need it. Her eyes looked like beautiful flowers on her face.

"You look gorgeous, so ya do," I told her as soon as I saw her.

"Ye aren't so bad yourself."

I smiled and then I took out a cigarette. I offered her one, but she said that nah, she was too clean for that stuff.

"The bar is just a wee dander that way," she said.

Then she started walking fast along the Falls, and I hurried to keep up. I kept me eye out for whoever might recognize me.

"So how was yer day, gorgeous?" I asked her after avoiding the eyes of a few mates across the road.

"Shite, really. I hate that job. But it's lookin' up now. How's you?"

"I'm grand. Spent my day thinking about you, really."

"Are ya this nice to all the girls?"

"Nah, only when they are as lovely as you."

Then she hit me on the shoulder, like she was pretending to be mad at me, but the hit had some bite behind it, let me tell ya.

"Only slagging!"

After that, conversation just flowed so naturally that I didn't even have to think before talking to her. Words just came out and I was being my total best self, and she thought I was interesting and funny and smart. It was just so easy, like.

And everything that she said, well, I just thought she was the most specialest and smartest person I'd ever met, and I just couldn't believe that such an amazing bird was wanting to talk to me as much as I was wanting to talk to her.

Finally, when we were almost right outside the bar, I asked her where she grew up and I found out she only grew up about five minutes from where I did, both on the outskirts of Derry city. It was a fucken' desolate slum to end all slums, but my perfect angel came from there too. It was crazy to say that flowers grow outta dirt, but it rang true with my Kate.

"It's too bad we only met now," I told her. I remember really wishing that I'd known her my whole life, thinking that maybe my whole life would've been different had I known her for all of it.

"I'm just happy we met at all." With that, she was through the door, and I was left standing on the sidewalk, heart beating through my chest.

I remember the concert was fucken' fantastic. The guy sounded like Van Morrison, mixed with Mick Jagger, with a bit of other-worldliness. He sang his own songs, which were very wild and almost crazy, like, and then he did covers of everyone's favourites, so it was like the perfect mix of new and old. The whole bar was up dancing by the end. I never heard of that guy again, though. Sometimes ya make it, sometimes ya don't, I guess.

I met a lot of Kate's mates that night. They were all well nice girls, very smart, and you could tell different (better!) than the crowd I ran with.

I felt this strange desire ta be better like them and forget everythin' in my own life, but it was fleeting, like. Maybe that was the thinkin' part startin' ta come back.

But anyway, all her mates really looked up ta her, and I could tell she was the unofficial leader, not because she wanted to be but because it was just so natural ta her.

I remember your man the singer started singing "Crazy Love" by Van, and the way he sang it, it almost had this rebellious and strong edge, like the way real, crazy love is. It's not sappy, or soft, it's scary as fuck and totally rebellious because you are going out on a scary fucken' whim and saying fuck it to everything in your head and only listening to what yer heart is telling you. If that ain't rebellious, I dunno wha is.

But when he started "Crazy Love," Kate grabbed my hand, and it was the first time and I remember thinking that it felt so perfect that I wanted to take glue and attach her to me forever. But she held my hand through the whole song, and squeezed it extra tight near the end, and after that, I can't remember a time that we were together when we weren't somehow connected. I never let go of her hand that night. I couldn't never look at her without wanting so bad to be touching her.

On that night, I felt free and weightless for the first time in as long as I could remember. I was happy, and nothing seemed to matter except right then.

Kate stirred somethin so fucken' powerful in me that after I'd met her I found it near impossible to think o' anything else. Which wasn't how I planned it, like, but once I had it, I sure as fuck didn't wanna change it.

Before I met Kate, I had a crap job and a crap life. After, I still had a crap job but it didn't matter anymore because now I had a great life. An unbelievably great life! Soon we spent every minute together. I'd visit her at work as much as I could. We'd eat sandwiches together for near every meal. We'd lay together on the wood floor because her back hurt after servin' for so many hours and she would talk to me about how she didn't want to just get married and have twelve Catholic children like her ma had, like her ma's ma had. She wanted more. She was the first person I'd met that I never got sick of.

I thought long and hard about what made Kate so well different from everyone else. It was like she was a soul from the future, transported into the wrong time, which was lucky for me but extremely unlucky for her. She had a certain consciousness to her that not many people here had. She could see all the bullshit. Most people just stood idly by for it, blinded by having seen no other way, and the others, like me, were responsible for it. You could really divide the lot of us into two worlds, like. But Kate, nah, like I said, she was from the other world. Tha older world, tha smarter world, tha world that felt a sickening pity for it all. She was above us. She was above me, and why she loved me I can'y tell you. World's biggest mystery.

Far more mysterious than Niagara fucken' Falls, believe me.

Very little is mysterious to me anymore. Up here, it's like you only got the same ten records to play all the time, and let me tell ya, even if they're great records, you are left bustin' for a radio station. Even a shite one because the great thrill in life is mystery. The mystery of not knowin' what's coming next, even if it is shite.

There are some perks to being up here, like. I get ta meet famous people. I met Elvis. I met John Lennon. I met Jesus, he's got gross hair in person. But ya know what they all said?

"I wish I wasn't fuckin' dead." Even *they* got regrets.

I got one big regret. Well, that's lies. There are lots, like, but there's one part that I continually think about regretfully, probably because it's the only part that could have been avoided.

I don't remember when we first said I love you. Far too pissed.

It was a Saturday night, and we had come home after a night out, where naturally I drank me face off. It was a class wee night with all her mates, right before Christmas. Christmas is real nice in Belfast, everything all done up honouring the Father's son, the few days' ceasefire and all that. But there was this real sad feeling underneath everything, which I can only think caused all me drinkin'.

A week earlier, fifteen Catholics, including two wee kids and two women, were killed by a bomb at this place called McGurk's Bar. At tha point it was by far the greatest loss of life that we'd ever seen, on either side. From the second I opened me eyes I felt the sick, angry, violent feeling and it vibrated all through me. When I was with Kate, I pushed it away, of course. But I knew there was going to be a retaliation, and I just couldn't believe they'd killed that many. (I didn't find out until I was up here that they were meant to take this IRA place called Gem's, but they picked McGurk's on the drive over because it was an easier target. Lazy, gutless fucks.)

When we got into my apartment it was flipping Baltic, like. The heat in that shithole was never workin', which was flaming ridiculous considering Belfast's winters are a damp, cruel mistress. Anyway, Kate got into the apartment and she wouldn't take her coat off even though it was fucken' covered in snow.

"Baby, I'm flamin' cold," she kept saying.

"I know, darlin'. Here, come into bed with me. I'll warm ya," and then I winked at her.

"Nah, it's too cold to take my coat off. Come and hug me."

"Yer coat is fucken' soaked. I'm not comin' to hug you, I'll be drenched."

"Fine," she said and then she did this fake pout she used to do that she thought was hilarious. So she'd be trying to do a frown-y face while laughing her wee ass off, which actually was a funny sight. So a'course, I started laughin' too.

"Ya know you leave me no choice," she told me while laughin' like a wild woman, half drunk and half just mad as a hatter as she was.

"No choice but to what?"

"You know," and then she started bopping around a bit.

"NAH!" I hollered.

"Yes!" And then she started doing what she called the "Hug Me!" dance, which she did whenever she wanted a hug and I couldn't give her one, like when I was busy, or already snug in bed or drainin' me python, or some other time when reasonable people didn't hug. And she did this dance wherever her heart pleased! She wasn't bothered if a million people could see her.

Luckily, that night it was just me.

Eventually, after I was done pissing myself laughing, I got up to hug her, half because I was worried she's wreck the place or kill herself. Only when she was tight in my arms did she stop the "Hug Me!" dance, so wranglin' her into position was a challenge, let me tell ya.

This is where I cut in and out. I remember telling her I loved her, but I didn't remember how it came up, which she found hysterical the next day.

"I tricked ye inta sayin' it! That's how!"

"Wha? Ye tricked me?" I asked.

"Ya were bustin' ta say it."

"Well, yer right I was."

And I was busting to say it from the moment I met her. So even if she was tricking me, I know I was thinking it at that very moment.

"That's better," she said.

"Oh yeah? I'm soaking now. Yer mad, so ya are."

"And you love it."

"I do," I said, feelin' the faggot-y nervousness in my voice.

"Ya do what?"

And then I knew for sure what she was getting it. I had no choice but ta be honest.

"Love you. I do love you."

"Ya do?" she said, surprisedlike, but also she looked so happy, and she smiled her gorgeous smile so wide. I just thought, How did I get lucky enough to make a bird like her so happy?

"I do," I said again.

"I love you too," she said, and then I could tell she meant it because she had a different look in her violet eyes than I'd seen before and I could tell that we'd gone to a deeper level than we were a second previous, and I knew that this was a moment I wanted to hold on to for as long as I humanly could.

After that she dragged me to the bed, and I remember thinking I'd never felt closer to God than I did when we were making love.

As I fell asleep, I held her. The world felt so slow. I told myself, "Don't let this go."

"Don't let this go," I whispered out loud, to prove to myself that everything I was feeling was real. The small words hung in the air, a reminder that I finally had something worth holding on to.

Her.

The memories aren't all perfect, though, like. She was always perfect, like, or pretty close, maybe too moany some days, but mainly perfect. I wasn't perfect. And sometimes lyin' ta her got tricky.

I remember I was pickin' her up from work one day, and I had been asked ta beat a man within an inch of his life the night before. Naturally, I did because tha's what ya did. I was proud of it then. The higher-ups liked my good work coz I had done wha they asked me.

It was like I became a different person when I was doin' that job. I had me "office" self and me real self when I was with her. The two never intersected, and sometimes I'm surprised at my ability to have two such different people within me.

Anyway, I was pickin' her up, and she noticed that me knuckles were bloodied.

"Wha happen'd there?" she asked.

"Ah, nothin'," I said.

"Tell me. Now."

"Ah, it was nothin'. Just got into a wee fight last night with a prick. Tha's all."

"Where were ya?"

"Jus tha wee place I took ya last week," I told her, thinkin' on my feet.

"Ya told me you were with yer mate Charlie at his."

"Yeah, well, we started at his and then we dandered way over there."

She didn't say nothin' after that, but she looked at me like I was the biggest liar she'd ever met. But in my mind, I was doing her a favour.

If ya think that being involved tore me up while we were together, you're wrong. I couldn't picture a life without it, even with my beautiful bird in it. I couldn't really just up and quit now, could I? Nah. While we were together I just kept doin' whatever they asked me, with no real thought. Small tasks, mainly like. I carried on, happy as hell, unchanged.

It's only now I ponder if I could have stopped.

I came home one night to her lying on the floor of my apartment, wailing.

"What's wrong?"

She moved, startled to see me, like she hadn't heard me dander in. She was lost in something bad and she looked at me like she wanted out of it, like I had to help her. I asked what was wrong again.

"They took Charlotte's husband, Camren."

Charlotte was her best mate. Her man was a provo, like me. I didn't know him much but to say hello. I had a sinking feeling in my gut. He wasn't the first man I'd known to be taken and definitely not the last.

"Who took him? Why?" I was playing dumb and I don't know why.

"Some Brit soldiers. Charlotte's been screaming since they raided the house, no one can calm her down. He is in jail, they'll probably kill him. She's got a wee baby inside her."

I never seen her more scared. I stayed silent then. I could feel the tension building in the air, and I knew what was coming. That's how connected we were. I could telepathically feel what she was raring to say to me.

"You're going to do this to me too."

"Nah, nah. They won't. They'd have no reason."

"Sean, they're taking all of you's. Ye need to get out. I can't have them take you too." I think even she knew that wasn't possible.

She turned her head away from me, lying flat on her back. Mad, like. I didn't know wha ta say. I was worried. Worried because now that she knew it was dangerous for her, and worried she'd leave me.

"They take you, I'll be alone. Then how much stronger are we? Women left without men? He's going to die in there, Sean. They're going to kill us all."

"Yer wrong."

You know that thinking part? It was well back at this point. The thinking part that I had aborted was kicking and screaming its way around my brain again.

"Kate, this is how it is. I can't stand by and do nothin'. I got no other choice."

I remember feeling so utterly gutted at this point. I felt so fucked. Like Romeo and Juliet or other star-crossed lovers that were just fucked from the get-go but it wasn't really their faults.

"So yer leaving me?" I asked her, almost afraid to even fill the air around me with that thought.

"Sometimes . . . sometimes at night when yer sleeping I tell myself to get up and leave and never come back."

This was my nightmare.

"Then I feel like my body is glued to yer sheets. I wish it were different."

So did I, but it wasn't, like. We both had scars on our hearts that would never heal.

"I am going to stay faithful to ye until the day I die," she told me.

We sat in together, until the sun set and until the moon went to half. Then we started to kiss.

"Let's move to Canada. Promise me we'll move to Canada," she whispered.

We had five months after that.

A lot changed. I gave her a ring, we were goin' to be tryin' for babies, all that.

Ya know, I could fill every page in this book with happy memories of us, what happened when we got engaged, fuck, how she looked in the morning time when she'd just woken up, but I'll spare us that. It's just too fucken' sad.

But if yer curious, like, everything in those next five months unfolded naturally and perfectly. We fell more and more in love with each passing hour, each passing second, really. Every night before I went ta sleep she'd kiss me and tell me that she'd be faithful ta me for the rest of her life. And in tha time we were together, the pain o' my brother, the weight of the war, the sadness that was Northern Ireland, it faded a little each day. She was my soul mate, we were two of a kind, and I know beyond a shadow of a doubt that we woulda been happy for the rest of our days. An' I know that she loved the shit out of me, almost as much as I loved her.

The last time I kissed her goodbye, she thought I was meetin' Couch at the pub. I still think it was best tha way.

I'd been asked ta do something real small, to just beat up some thug that was botherin' someone's wee brother, and I didn't think nothin' of it. I said, Yeah, of course, and figured I'd be back before night fell.

The irony is that this wasn't even my own doin'. I was just in the wrong place at the wrong time.

I was walkin' up Victoria Street on my way, and the air smelled of the sea and faintly rusting shipyards of Belfast Lough. It was half four, but it was already dark. Night always falls early on winter's nights in Belfast and morning dawns slowly. The city was bathed in this yellow sulphur light, and I remember thinkin' tha I was cold and wishin' I was snug somewhere with Kate.

And those were my last living thoughts.

The sidewalk around me shook with enormous force, and a wave of searing air rushed over me. It lifted me from my feet, and for a second too long I could see it all around me; building comin' down, people catchin' fire, blood, people screamin', horrible screamin' everywhere. I'm not sure how I landed, I lost all sense of up and down. But soon I was coffin'd in debris, like, and it crushed me, heavy. I opened my mouth to speak, to yell for Kate, but I only found more debris chokin' me. And then my mouth filled with blood.

Ya wanna know the funny part? My side planted the bomb.

I watch her from up here, I rarely stop watchin' her, she's like a real good TV channel I never wanna turn off. She knows I watch her too. We don't have conversations, like. That's not really possible, but she knows I'm listening.

And I know like my tattoo, that useless provo scrolled across my back, Tiocfaidh ár lá.

Our day will come.

Swelter

My friend Colin died the summer we all turned seventeen.

It happened on a Tuesday. A Tuesday of all days. What ever happens on a Tuesday? What ever happens on any day? When I heard, I was helping my kid sister, Sarah, fix her bike. She was eleven. I was the last to know.

I'm Louise. I hate that name, but it's not like I picked it. My other option is Sugar Tits, so said Colin. I chose Louise.

I'm blond and grossly skinny, way too skinny. Not even in a model way. Sometimes I'm not bad. Whenever things are going well, I start to feel vain. Then something like this happens and I'm ugly all over again.

There were four of us until Colin died. We made a funny-looking crew. Hedge, short for Tom, is fat and short. You know me. Then there's Seb. He's stupid good-looking, but I'm the only one who thinks so. And Colin, normal height and skinny like me with grey eyes and a new hair colour every three weeks. We called ourselves T.L.C., The Legend Crew. Don't ask me why, it's not like any of us ever did anything legendary.

People always ask why I only hang out with guys. I don't have a reason. The truth is that it's funny who you feel the most like yourself around.

When I heard, it was one of those days in late August when heat radiates off the pavement and you can see it, before your eyes, like little waves of air, I remember them clear as a bell the day I heard, feeling the gravity bend before my eyes.

My sister started crying hysterically. Colin was always her favourite. He was really quiet, but he was cool with little kids. "Kids don't really need to talk," he said once. "Adults pollute everything with talking."

You want to know the first thing I thought? Shit, he made it to everybody's birthday party but mine. That's a selfish thing to think, isn't it?, but that's the first thing I thought. Sometimes I can't even believe myself. Jesus.

He died in the most badass and tragic way. He did a lot of graffiti, huge, crazy, angry murals all over the place. Normally he'd do them really late at night and he'd come wake you up at six in the morning and you'd have to bike over to wherever he'd worked the whole night before. It was really annoying, but you'd forgive him because he'd have this Jack Nicholson smile on his face. And the murals were truly gangster.

Beautiful colours, weird shapes, funny words all sewn together on some wall in the middle of town. It would really piss old people off when they'd see it, but we were the only ones who knew the culprit, so, natch, he never got caught.

Anyway, in the middle of summer, he'd taken to working all night on boxcars at the train tracks. It was dawn when it happened. It was his own stupid fault. He had his earphones in. Fucking idiot. A train came at dawn, and he never even heard it. If he didn't have his ears in, he would have moved. Instead, it was done, just like that.

I feel split up. Half of me thinks if he had to go, at least he went doing what he loved best. But then one morning in the middle of work after I'd been up all night thinking, I thought about how much it would have hurt to go like that. Sure, it was short, but it must have really hurt. After I realized that, I lost it, snot everywhere, and my boss at the deli counter let me leave early even though I never told him what happened.

Maybe he knew. It's funny how word spreads when a kid dies.

I couldn't bring myself to go see the mural. The boys did. When I asked him how it looked, they said, "Cool," and that's all. So I figured I'd leave it at that.

Like I said, it's fucked up when a kid dies.

The funeral was held at some church in the middle of town. Colin would have hated it. It was filled with people he didn't even know, and even if he had known them, he still would have fucking hated it.

We, the only people he did know and usually didn't hate, weren't involved at all. Seb and Hedge asked his parents if they could be pallbearers, because my dad told them that'd be the thing to do, but they couldn't get a straight answer. A little later, I asked if I could read a poem I'd written about something cheesy, like summer turning to winter, and all they said was, "Thanks for the sentiment."

I can't blame them, though. Just imagine how you'd be if your kid died. I'm surprised they didn't come into the church with guns and shoot everybody just to make some sense out of the fucked-up fact that we'd all lived, for no reason, when their kid had died. That would be true vigilante justice and I don't even think they'd deserve jail for it.

The funeral felt really long, like it stretched out for hours, days, weeks, months, years, like it covered miles, countries, continents, oceans, and equators. The heaviness that sits on a bunch of people who are mourning the death of a young person weighs trillions of pounds and crushes your bones. I just got tattooed on my ankle and it says, *Inside each man there is a poet who died young.* Colin died when he was still the poet, but after he died, that poet died in me, that poet died in us all. We felt the poems dying that day. Growing up is realizing that everything about life is unfair, and the most unfair part is that it ends. Life kicked the childhood out of me that day. Once you're gone, you really can't go back.

The reverend talked some shit about the loons on the lake at his cottage, about Jesus, about how Colin loved boating and how the peace he found on the water would be the same peace he found in the Hereafter. That was so ridiculous I laughed out loud until my mom slapped me to shut up. His dad owned a boat that he used to invite girls from our high school onto when he was drunk at Colin's birthday parties. The last time Colin had been on the boat he puked all over me because he'd pounded a bottle of peach schnapps twenty minutes earlier. He hated that fucking boat. But no one remembers the truth when you're dead.

I couldn't get out of the church fast enough.

"Colin's got the right idea," Hedge whispered to me when we were walking out, like kids following leaders, in the funeral procession.

"What?" I whispered as quietly as I could, like if anyone heard me speak they would think I was so disrespectful that they'd kick me out of town forever and I'd have to live in a cardboard box on the desolate border between here and the next Bumfuck, Nowhere, town.

"The only way to stay immortal is to die young," he said, way too loud. "That way, people remember you for what you could have been, not for what you ended up as. I want to be forever young too."

What is there to say to somebody when he believes something as crazy as that?

I found Seb. My first thoughts upon seeing him were, yet again, selfish. Fuck, he looked good in a suit.

"Do you feel different?" Seb asked me. His eyes looked so damn blue right then.

I shrugged. What a ridiculous question. *Of course I felt different.* Then I motioned for the boys to meet me in the parking lot. Sitting on some random car, I took a dime out of my purse and rolled us a fat joint.

We knew we were smoking to Colin, but who was ready to say it? The weed wasn't very good.

A few minutes later, Hedge had to leave because his mom found us smoking the joint and screamed at him, "This is a time for families!"

So then it was just Seb and me.

"Want to come to my place?" he asked.

We ended up in his bedroom. He pushed me up against his wall and he kissed me. He'd kissed me before, always at parties when he was drunk or high, but this time, it felt different. He meant it this time. He tasted like those white tic tacs, kind of vanilla and kind of mint. Pure delicious. I knew then he'd planned it.

"Let me move in you," he whispered in my ear.

And before I knew it we were having sex, real sex, for my first time ever.

When he finished, I'll be honest, not that long after we started, he kissed me, really tender, like boys always kiss girls in movies and rarely in real life.

"I love you, Louise," he said before we had to put our clothes on because his parents got home. I felt so pretty when he said that. I started crying and then I couldn't stop.

Seb let me sit on the handlebars of his bike and drove me home the long way. It would have been awkward sticking around his house with his parents home. I could hear his mom crying too when we snuck out the back window. So instead, we drove through town dressed all in black, like morbid Amish people during a parade. All I needed was a bonnet.

Later that night, I wondered if he made love to me because he wanted to feel closer to Colin. Then I thought, maybe we'll get married because we have this in common. No one else is going to know Colin, not how we did, and by pledging ourselves to each other for eternity, we would, in some ways, be staying close to Colin forever.

Funny how history works.

Four days later it was my birthday party. I didn't feel like a big celebration, but the boys told me I was being weak if I didn't do something. I knew the score; they just wanted to get shitfaced for a reason. What kind of a friend would I be if I denied them an opportunity to get drunk? Reasons were usually so few and far between.

We sat on the rocks near the water where we would always meet every Saturday night for the remainder of our adolescent lives. Hedge smoked me on a joint, and Seb told me that he got me something but he'd forgotten it at home.

"Tell me now."

"No, shut up."

"Tell me now or I'll leave and never come back." God, I can be a real selfish bitch sometimes.

And then when Hedge wasn't looking he whispered, "It's romantic, okay?"

As Bob Dylan once said, we started out on burgundy then soon hit the harder stuff. I shouldn't have let them do that because sometime around midnight Hedge threw a small rock at Seb. It was totally out of nowhere, like when George Bush just plum didn't help the black people in New Orleans.

"What the fuck?" Seb screamed, throwing another bigger rock.

"Stop, you guys!" I yelled.

Then before I knew it, they were punching each other, so hard. I'd seen them play-fight before, but this time they were truly going at each other, vicious. I started crying because I felt so helpless. God, being a girl is helpless sometimes and it really pisses me off. I kept screaming at them but they didn't even look at me. Then Seb's nose started bleeding and Hedge fell to the ground like he couldn't breathe. I had never felt so panicked in my whole life.

Then do you know what those assholes did? They started laughing! Laughing like maniacs. Then they picked up sand and rocks and driftwood and threw it around, yelling like lunatics released from the asylum.

"FUCK THIS!"

"FUCK YES!"

"THE LEGEND CREW!"

Then Hedge started crying, really hard, and I'd never seen him cry before. Seb walked up to him and they hugged each other. A few seconds later, they started wrecking shit again. It was like a scene out of that terrible book everybody has to read in Grade 10, *Lord of the Flies*. I was just waiting for one of them to eat the other.

I left five minutes later and they didn't even see me go.

It really is true that men deal with things totally differently than women.

Seb came and found me the next morning.

"Sorry," he said from my doorstep.

"You look like shit."

"Can I come in?"

I moved aside. Now that he'd been inside me, I acted totally different around him. It is a universal girl law that you can never act normal when you want to. I felt like my mouth was chicken-wired shut. There were about eighty-five things I wanted to say to him, but they were lazy fucks and just refused to slide from my brain to my lips.

"So . . . I brought you your birthday gift."

It was a mix CD.

"Should I listen to it now?"

"Yeah, if you want."

I put it on, and we sat on my couch. The house felt cold, like fall decided to just show up that day, like when your aunt from out of town comes by for no reason and then you later realize it's because she's getting divorced. But with Seb next to me, I began to feel warmer. I had goosebumps, but I was sure I was also sweating.

"Why are all the songs in French?"

"Because I'm moving there."

"What?"

"In six months, I'm moving to Paris."

"You are?"

"Come with me."

I started laughing, like I knew he was kidding.

"I hate it here. You do too."

"You're serious?"

"Yes. Colin hated it here and he never got to leave. Remember how he'd talk about getting a passport and taking off to Europe and he'd have that obscenely hopeful look on his face?"

I did remember.

"Well, we get to leave. There's nothing keeping us here. I want to go and I want you to come with me."

"But we don't speak French."

"I think everyone speaks English there anyway."

He kissed me, and once I started kissing him back I couldn't stop. We spent the rest of the day kissing and then talking about French things like cheese and wine and the Eiffel Tower and Ernest Hemingway in the 1920s.

He ran his hands through my hair, and I fell asleep on his chest, listening to his heartbeat, dreaming about France and Europe and London and Big Ben, places I thought I'd never see.

I lay out in my backyard the next morning. I was alone. My parents had gone to work. The sun felt nice on my skin, but I was still cold and I couldn't shake it.

I had my headphones on. I listened to the CD Francais, as I had taken to calling it. The music pushed the leaves from the trees, the clouds from the sky, the blue from heaven, and I could see all the planets. I could see silvery Pluto, beautiful red Jupiter, and then yellow Venus. I could see the infinite blackness and all the beautiful orbs of colours that populated it. I reached out and touched Neptune. It felt like cold water.

I think I even saw Colin waving at me.

"This town is so severe and silent. I wonder if a person can die from it, choking to death on things they always wanted to but were never able to say." Colin told me that the week before he died. We'd just gone out for breakfast, the two of us, because everyone else had slept through their alarms.

It was a pretty insignificant thing, coming from him. He always said shit about life and death, waxed poetic about unanswerable bullshit. The boys called him Socracock.

It's only because he's gone that all those trivial things from the past echo on and on and on, but I wonder if maybe it was the silence that killed him. Maybe he had died, choking on the silence, seconds before the train hit him. So on his death certificate it should have said that the cause was "peace and quiet," not railroad misadventure.

When I went inside, still shivering, I put the kettle on.

The water boiled while the day was on fire, and I watched it, patiently waiting like a bird on a wire.

Monster

I am a monster.

This is how I was born, a fault in my stars. I can do no more to change it than an old dog can trade his worn, dirty fur for the clean feathers of a baby bird just because he dreams of taking flight.

I can only really breathe when I am alone. Sometimes, in these moments, I think of James, the man who loves me, the man who will marry me next month, and I feel cruel. He does not know that I was born wearing the blue uniform of a prisoner inside myself. Everything else feels like a costume.

Especially that white dress.

I get on my knees and pray that I have a fighting chance.

I started killing animals when I was five.

It was around then that I began the long, solitary walks around our property. My mother never seemed bothered by my absences. She was a woman preoccupied by herself only. She spent her days tanning her lithe body and having gentlemen other than my father over.

"Just friends." I was jealous of her. I saw how men looked at her and I wanted that same attention myself. How does a five-year-old covet that specific and twisted breed of sex?

I saw a bird on the side of the road. It had a broken wing, and it was yelling. I didn't recognize that it was in pain, only that it was helpless. I lifted my shoe and I felt it's wing break beneath me. I remember feeling it move, how it wanted to fly, hearing it scream, the struggle and then the collapse.

Suddenly, I was not angry anymore. I was not happy. I was not anything. I was calm for the first time, and all I wanted was to recreate that feeling again and again.

I wasn't particular: mice I caught, any bug, any living creature I could get my hands on. Birds were always difficult. When I was eight, I killed a neighbourhood dog. Seeing the MISSING signs, I felt no guilt, only stupid for being so brazen. I considered myself lucky that I was never found out and was not so obvious again.

I knew there was something wrong with my behaviour, my compulsions. I cried once to my mother about it.

"Stop making up stories," she said.

I learned to shave my legs when I was ten. I lost my virginity when I was eleven to a seventeen-year-old boy. I developed early, I could lie and pass for fifteen.

Suddenly, almost overnight, men had become my act of violence. I've had so many I've lost count. James is the first man I have fooled for a long time, the only man who has promised to take care of me.

I've grown old and my looks have faded, I wear my promiscuity like a memory, a stale perfume that I can't wash of my body.

How do you begin today with all of yesterday still inside you?

Sometimes, still, I'll catch a mouse and take great pleasure in crushing it with my fist. Bodily fluids do not move me; blood, semen, tears—none of these weigh heavy on me.

As the big day approaches, I find myself studying James when he is asleep. He looks so helpless. More helpless than I could ever be in the most dire of situations, and this helplessness radiates off him in his sleep. Looking at him, I feel like a monster in a fairy tale: hairy, yellow-eyed, and mute. I want to crush him like that bird, sit on him until he suffocates.

When I wake from these spells I am horrified because I thought I knew better than this.

I promise myself daily that I will be discreet and that I will only take other men when I feel like I'm drowning. I will be a good wife to James.

I repeat this to myself over and over, hoping, somehow to believe it.

Some nights, I feel so torn that I cannot share a bed with him and sleep alone on the wood floor beneath him.

He is taking me on a getaway this weekend; "some time alone before the wedding," he told me.

"Isn't it beautiful?" he asks, waking me from a sleep that until now I wasn't certain I had fallen into.

I look out the window of our red Ford truck that's covered in road dust. I lift my head and straighten my shoulders to get a better look at what's on the other side of the glass. The clear, hard sky stretches for miles. Mountains, presidential in the distance, dwarf every tree and farm around them. It is breathtaking. Being around so much space I feel myself wanting to wander like a lonely buffalo.

"Baby?" he asks.

I had forgotten James was in the car with me.

"Yes, beautiful," I tell him. My accent is barbed with the softness only sharpshooters can imitate, sounds different in my own head, when I am alive in thought, than it does when I speak to him, dead in conversation. I don't understand where the pretense comes from, but I am being dishonest with my voice when I speak, except within the confines of my own skull. My real drawl is lower, has more gruffness, and a depth that I don't share with anyone, guarded like jewels.

He smiles at me, and then he puts his hand on mine, and I keep it there until the car stops. That is what normal people who are in love do.

If I can convince him, how far behind am I?

When the car stops, James and I bring our luggage to the front door of the cabin. As I slam the trunk, I feel his hand graze my ass.

We are kissing on the doorstep now, and I feel his excitement, about us, about the future, about everything that life offers most people. His hands travel all over my body, with an increasing pressure, and for a moment I feel sad. I have never felt excited, not like that, about anything in my life. I can mimic excitement, as I am now, by mirroring his actions, putting my hands on his body where he puts his on mine.

But right now my body acts like an orchard of bones. James takes my hand and leads me through the cabin up the stairs to our bedroom. He lays me down and undresses me. His touch is soft and I am used to it.

"You feel so good," I tell him.

I am not lying. He does feel good. He is different than the other men. We are gentle with each other where they used to bruise me, bite me, make me bleed. Usually, I hide my body from James until my map of scars, traces of the other men are gone.

When I look untouched, like now, our bodies fit together well, like pieces of a jigsaw puzzle. It doesn't feel satisfying, only like kindness's sister. He cups my left breast in his hand. I wrap my legs around him. We begin.

As he thrusts himself inside me, I smile at him, trying to force myself into a dream—a state to silence the private voice in my head. That voice thinks it's writing my story as the narrator, as the double, secret-sharer of my existence. But in truth, there is no duality. I am that voice, and the person that I pretend to be only exists when there's a stage.

"You're so wet." I run my hand along his back.

He is speeding up now. His rhythmic motion calms me, feels natural, like cylindrical parts of machinery finding their cogs. I know it will end soon, but I don't want it to, feeling like I could fall asleep and stay that way forever if only he could continue until his heart stopped.

It's working, I tell myself. This is working.

"I love you," he tells me. My James has loved me, intimately, since the moment he laid eyes on me. No other man has ever loved me like that. I have long wondered if that was because somehow James knew, though not consciously thought, that I could never love him and, attracted to that calamity, threw himself against me.

"I love you too," I say back but sound so hollow that I wonder how he can believe it.

When he rolls off me, I lean to the side, placing my back against his front. He holds me tightly. Too tightly. I'm suffocating.

"I can't wait until you're my wife."

I reach around my body, hold his hands, and also hold myself, further shortening my own breath.

The new moon rode high over the modest golden fields and bruised skyline. Too hot, tangled in sheets and sweating, I left the bed frustrated, wanting for sleep but unable to find it. I needed to walk. The space I create cutting through the thick air is cooling, and when I am far enough from James I can breathe again.

How could I think this was working?

Since he proposed marriage, my hair has been falling out. All around the house I see it, like small golden chains, littering the floor. No matter how much I sweep, I cannot clear them away. The strands multiply each day. They are little lightning bolts made of my dead cells that mock me and remind me there's a reason that actresses wear wigs. I wonder if a bald bride is still a beautiful one.

My mother died last year, bald. I know now that she was faced with this same decision. She chose to marry my father. She gave him forever within the numbered days.

I wonder if it cost her life; the cancer sprouting everywhere it could, seeping into her bones, punishing her for lying. Sometimes, I want to ask her what to do, even though I know it's ridiculous to believe a dead person can hear you.

My mother watched me as I got older. She knew that we were two of a kind, that she had given birth to herself. She was jealous of me, my youth and beauty, but I was her accomplice. She'd tell me the truth and I would cover for her. She would leave for hours to visit with friends who did not exist. I told my father she was seeing Mary, her friend from church, who never attended when we did. There was her doctor, Mr. Green, whose office did not exist in the phonebook. And there was Mrs. Merriweather, the sick old widow to whom mother would bring dinner every Saturday night, to an address I made up, that did not exist any-where in Texas.

"You and me, we're liars. That's not so bad. Anyone who tells you they aren't is a worse type than we are." That was one of the kinder things my mother ever said to me. I was not loved by my mother, but she did claim me as her own.

I lie to James almost constantly. Most of the lies are meaningless, it's just that telling the truth feels so flaccid.

Lately, I have started telling him I am seeing a psychiatrist when really I cannot think of anything more pointless. For three hours every week I drive as far away as I can before I have to turn back, giving my face a break from its metalled mask.

He does not know that I have seen dozens of therapists but after two or three sessions, I never return.

I walk home through such blackness that I cannot see two paces in front of me. I dread each step closer to the cabin knowing I will not sleep tonight. There is no extra blanket for my wooden mattress.

"Should I get a six-pack? Or enough for us both?"

It is now noon, and we are among the yahoos at the local grocery store. James will drink the beer as soon as we get home. He thinks it's celebratory. I do not. So, I shake my head: no, I don't want any.

Alcohol rarely passes my lips and I never get drunk. Alcohol provides James an escape, I guess. But it is my belief that escaping through alcohol allows people to remain stuck in lives they hate. I believe that if you are unhappy, you might as well know it, and know it always.

Three children are in line in front of us, buying candy. They are arguing over who will pay the fifty-seven cents for their sweets made of pink, thick chalk.

"You said you'd get it, Laura! I got it last week!" says the first one.

"NO, I did! Stop lying, you liar!" says the second.

"You're all stupid!" says the third.

I will lose my mind if this continues.

"I'll get it," I tell the older lady at the register. I lay the quarters, a nickel, and two pennies on the counter. The sound of metal hitting metal hurts my ears.

On the way out James grabs my hand and rubs my index finger slowly with his rough thumb.

"You will be the most wonderful mother."

"I can't wait," I say, smiling.

I know beyond a shadow of a doubt that I will not have his children. I will take birth control pills until the day that I die.

Not having children raises fewer questions than never marrying.

On the way back home, I did make my decision.

I was in the same position that I was on the drive there, only reversed. Everything was exactly the same. We listened to the same music, his hand was resting on mine, and I was staring at the hard, blue sky above me out the dirty window, and in the nowhere and everywhere moment, I felt so cruel I swore I bled.

I wanted to pick a fight with him. A desperate scrap. I am a useless old boxer with a bum shoulder, fighting to prove that I can still hurt.

I looked over at him. He caught me staring. He smiled at me so broadly, and like skies after thunder, the light grew.

I knew in that moment that he loved me more than he could ever love anyone. He was committed to me. Tangled, matted so deeply. He looked so natural, so serene, as if he was made, created solely, to meet his maker. He would never get out alive.

"I can't do it."

"Do what, baby?" he said.

He looked at me, still serene, unmoved. I searched his face for any sign that he knew what I was saying. There was none.

"What's wrong, baby?"

I look away, and I feel all alone in the car next to him. The loneliness invites breath back in me. He will never know that we are strangers. I can lie to him until we both turn to dust, and he will never know.

Why did I think that I needed to change?

It is winter now, and the wind shakes the bare branches above me.

I walk on cobblestone. I am not used to the heaviness that I am carrying with me.

I reach the end of the path. I look backward.

He lifts my veil. The brisk winter air slaps my face like angry hands.

A few moments later, we are pronounced man and wife.

Saturday

A week before Joe died, Meryl had an appointment with his doctor, Aaron Stein. St. Mary's Hospital was not where Meryl had worked, in palliative care, as a grief counsellor for twenty-three years. She had worked for Johns Hopkins.

St. Mary's was the hospital closest to her house, and it had the best specialists for what Joe needed. Through the years she had made some friends there, but now no one told her anything. All she could find out was that Dr. Stein was new there.

Meryl didn't like him.

He was young, around thirty. He was handsome, broad, and muscled. She had never found it so difficult to like such a good-looking man.

She hated his voice. He spoke so quickly that he was winded by the end of each appointment. The pace made it hard to take in everything. Between his gasps and run-on sentences, she got lost.

Still, in the two years he had been Joe's doctor, Meryl never asked him to speak slower.

The irony. Now she was the little old lady whose husband was dying, who couldn't understand what the doctor was saying.

"You help people die, how can you be confused?" she'd ask herself as she left his office, dizzy every time.

But on that day a week before Joe died, she felt dizzy as she walked into his office. She knew how this appointment would go. Joe had stopped eating.

She sat like she used to sit when she was a nervous girl, with her hands pressed firmly on the chair, underneath her thighs.

Dr. Stein was ten minutes late.

She looked around his office. There was a white rug, a white desk, white lamps. What type of a person would want an office this white? Wouldn't it get dirty?

Meryl noticed a picture on his white desk that she had never seen before: two small children and a young woman, smiling. She got out of her chair and inched closer to the picture, staring at these happy people. She wondered how long he had been married. How old were these children? Her nose was almost to the glass when Dr. Stein came into the room.

"Hello, Mrs. Johnson."

Meryl turned around quickly, trying to appear as if she hadn't been snooping.

"Lovely family. Your wife is just beautiful."

"Oh no, that's my sister and her kids. I'm not married."

Figures.

Meryl sat back down in her chair, promising herself that today she would force herself to take in everything Dr. Stein said.

"Beautiful day, isn't it?" Dr. Stein said, busying himself with papers, turning his back to her.

"Yes, it's lovely out."

"Did you have a chance to get out and enjoy it at all?"

"No, not yet. Maybe this afternoon."

"That will be nice."

"Yes, I think so."

Dr. Stein turned, looked at Meryl, and slowly put his papers down. He never moved as quickly as he spoke.

"So we have the test results here."

Meryl nodded.

"Joe has enough cancer in him to kill five men. It's time to say goodbye."

For a still minute, the doctor stood, and Meryl sat, in tableau.

"Why is your office so white?" she asked.

Even when you know that bad news is coming, it's still disappointing. Even when you know there is no hope, a small part of you believes that you will get that miracle, that things could still turn around.

It's why battered women stand by their husbands, why failed actors don't leave Los Angeles, and why Meryl sat in Dr. Stein's office on that Friday, disappointed and surprised.

"You're very handsome, Joe, did you know that?"

Meryl stood in the kitchen, washing dishes. It was one of those days early in the spring when you open the front door, ignoring that it's too early to celebrate the season.

She looked over her shoulder at Joe, who was lying on the daybed that Meryl had fixed for him in the kitchen.

"Even like this?" he asked.

"Yes, even like that."

Joe watched Meryl and the soft circles her shoulders made as she did the dishes.

"You are still as beautiful as the day I married you."

He won't remember this in twenty minutes, Meryl told herself. She had a lot of experience with pain medication, and she knew it made people say things they didn't mean. She had watched so many families upset by how the drugs changed their loved ones. Mean, brutally honest, fearless. She would tell them it was the drugs talking. When the medication wore off, or when the doctors got the dosage right, they would come back.

She wanted Joe to come back.

Meryl felt the warm water fall over her hands, watched the soap foam over the dishes.

"That's not true, Joe. I'm not beautiful anymore."

"Yes it is, Meryl. You are beautiful."

As the morning light flooded the kitchen and hit her shoulder, making her warm, Meryl paused. Maybe he was complimenting her for the same reason she was complimenting him. She wanted to say nice things to him while she still could.

Joe had never been handsome.

He was tall and lanky, and had never found himself in his body. He started going bald young. He looked much older than he was. But when he smiled, his skin crinkled and his eyes closed and his whole face changed shape. If he smiled at you once, you remembered him for the rest of your life.

While she was drying her favourite mug, Meryl remembered how she was beautiful once. She turned back to her husband.

"I'm not like I was, Joe. Not anymore."

She knew her face once looked as if someone had spent a long time thinking it over, making her perfect. Now when she passed by the mirror, she didn't recognize the woman staring back.

Meryl finished drying the dishes and put them away in the cupboard above her. She stood on her toes, struggling to reach the higher shelves. It was something Joe would have helped her with.

"Are you comfortable?" she asked him.

"Very."

Then, after a moment, Joe said, "Meryl, come kiss me."

That was strange.

"Not now, Joe. I'm busy."

"Meryl, come kiss me like you used to."

He was slurring.

"I'm putting the dishes away."

"I don't care. Come close. Come kiss me. Like last week. Before I had to get you home to your father. Remember that? Come kiss me. Like last week."

Even though she knew better, the hazy moments between lucidity scared her.

"Joe, you're confused again. That wasn't last week."

Meryl was going to call that good-for-nothing doctor. He had given Joe too much oxycodone.

"Come here. Come kiss me."

They can be so stubborn.

Meryl put the plate down on the counter and crossed the tile floor to sit with Joe.

After a few seconds, she placed her hand on his chest and slowly moved her fingertips back and forth below his collarbone. Finally, she rested her palm on his left breast, remembering the many times she had fallen asleep just there. She leaned down, placed her lips on his lips, to remember how she kissed him when they were young.

She closed her eyes. In that moment, she felt again like the girl she used to be. But the moments where the past feels like the present are never long enough.

After only a few seconds, Joe's breathing became laboured. Meryl quickly raised herself up against his chest.

"What's wrong?"

She saw wetness in Joe's eyes. His face had changed and she knew he did not remember asking her to kiss him.

He let out a low moan.

"What's wrong, Joe? Why are you crying?"

"It hurts."

"What hurts? Where hurts?"

But there was no answer. The noises he made just got louder.

A week later that good-for-nothing doctor told her that it wasn't the medication.

The cancer was in his brain.

When they were young, the space between them was so charged that it took every part of Meryl to fight what her insides wanted. His power over her was his skin. He marked her bones.

"Take off your dress."

"No, Joe. I can't. Not here."

"Yes, you can."

Meryl looked up at him. Looking at him made her drunk. She was not used to feeling so out of control. When his body was pressed against hers, she felt both empty and full.

"I want you."

She felt him pressed up against her harder.

"I love you, Meryl."

When he moved in her, everything around her moved too. Images danced across the ceiling, shadows mixed slowly, choreographed.

When they finished, he lay on top of her. He held her so close, the heat between them radiated, and Meryl felt as if she was on fire.

"I should go, my darling."

He kissed her goodbye and touched her face more delicately than he ever had before.

Why was he touching her differently now? Had she done something wrong?

"I could get carried away with you," he whispered in her ear.

She looked up at him hovering over her. She wanted him against her again. She didn't like the space.

"Meryl, why do you look so sad?"

"I'm just tired."

He climbed out her window, his silhouette outlined by the dawn.

She cried after he was gone, for a long time, for no reason. She felt cold and then feverish.

She lay in her bed that whole day. She was alone but surrounded by the smell of him, haunted by his touch. When her father asked her if she wanted any food, she said she wasn't hungry. She didn't eat at all. And even though she was exhausted, she didn't sleep.

She was so scared, now that she couldn't be without him.

"What was he like?"

Meryl sat in St. Mary's atrium with Joe's nurse, Lori.

Lori was young and pretty. She had come from the Philippines three years ago and hadn't seen her children since she left. She told Meryl that one evening in passing, as if it wasn't unusual or heartbreaking. She showed Meryl pictures of her three children that night. They looked so young.

Meryl had always liked Lori, who let her stay late, past visiting hours, to sit with Joe. Meryl figured it was because Lori knew what it was like to sleep alone.

"Joe?"

"Yes, Joe, before he was here. What was he like?"

Meryl was at a loss.

"Wonderful."

"Was he funny? He seems funny."

That afternoon, in the hot atrium, as her sweater clung to her breast, Meryl remembered that, yes, Joe was funny.

"What did he do?"

"He was a teacher, actually."

"Did he like it?"

"Yes, he did. He was very patient. I think he missed it when he retired."

"What did he do when he wasn't working?"

"Are you always so curious about your patients, Lori?"

"No, just the ones I spend a lot of time with. Sorry. I'll stop."

"No, no, it's all right." The questions bothered Meryl.

She knew what Lori was doing. She had done it many times herself. She was trying to help Meryl grieve.

As sweat crept down the nape of her neck soon to curve down her spine, Meryl promised herself something. As soon as she got home, she was going to write a list of all the things that made Joe Joe. She was going to put the list in a bag. Then she would put it away in a drawer.

She wanted to write down the way he held his mystery books in bed every night, so close to his face, with a half-crooked smile. And how quickly he turned the pages, and how disappointed he was when they ended. The expression on his face when he'd roll his eyes at Meryl over some boring stranger's shoulder. Then how she would burst out laughing, and he would look back at her, pleased to have made her happy, grateful that she was stranded too. Or the way he fell asleep every night, on his side. How he couldn't settle until he put his hand on her hip.

"So?" asked Lori. "What did he do when he wasn't working?"

"Well, regular things. He liked watching baseball. His favourite team was our team, the Orioles. And it never bothered him that they always lost. Every spring he would watch the games and still believe that they could win."

Meryl had to write down everything she could. That way she could answer properly the next time someone asked her what her husband was like.

When he was gone.

My darling Meryl,

It is late now, and you are sleeping in the next room. You went to bed angry at me, for some reason that I couldn't understand, but that I knew was right. When you were yelling at me, all I wanted was to write you this. I am cautious now.

I have this vision of you in my head, the night I met you across that bar, laughing so loudly. Your laughter was so bold, and you were so striking. I was taken with you immediately. I knew then that nothing would be the same.

Time passes swiftly, and here we are, a few years in. You get angry at me for holding back, for not being honest, for not saying what you deserve to hear. You are right to be angry with me. I scare you with my silence. But I don't mean to.

Some days, I look at you, and I am overwhelmed by all that I feel. I find a catch in my throat. You don't know.

I need you to know that I can't lose you. Please know that when you think you have lost me, I am not gone, only waiting to be found.

I love you.

Marry me.

Joe.

Meryl had always struggled with insomnia, but since Joe's diagnosis she found herself awake more than ever. Every night she would lie in her bed in the darkness, her eyes closed, not sleeping.

It wasn't dreams that woke her. It wasn't restlessness. It was questions, twisting and turning around in her head.

What appointments did Joe have tomorrow? What did Mrs. Anderson say about her sister's husband who had the same cancer? Would Joe be well enough to go to the dinner they said yes to months ago?

Why did this happen?

She had watched this same situation play out hundreds of times. Throughout her career, Meryl silently thought that families were lucky if they could see it coming. But it looked so different projected against those long, aching nights.

Not half past three, she'd think.

"It can't be quarter after four," she'd tell herself.

"Oh no. Five to two," she'd whisper.

Ever since she was a small sleepless girl, Meryl hated knowing what time it was if she woke up in the middle of the night. She could never fall back asleep if she knew how long she had before she needed to be awake. Instead, Meryl would stay awake and count the seconds until the sun rose.

"Well, curiosity kills the cat," she'd say.

Then one night, at around ten after four, after weeks of thinking in the black, she knew the answer.

She would rather have Joe snatched from her than pulled away slowly.

There was no luxury in being able to say goodbye.

"Do you need to call anyone?" Lori asked Meryl at 7:05, ten minutes after Joe died.

Meryl knew she had to call someone. She didn't know who.

"Do you want a tissue, Meryl?" asked Lori.

She turned and stared at Lori. She didn't know how long she looked at Lori before she answered that, yes, she wanted a tissue.

"Compose yourself, Meryl. You need to make a call, you just need to make it through this call," she told herself.

She picked up the telephone and dialled her closest friend Evelyn's number. As the phone rang, Meryl decided what she would say when Evelyn picked up.

"Hello?"

Meryl forgot what she had planned to say. What should she say?

"Hello?"

She had no idea what she should say.

"Hello? Hello?"

Say something. Say anything.

"Evelyn, it's Meryl. He's gone."

As the words came out of Meryl's mouth, she wished she had said them differently.

"Do you need anything?" asked Evelyn.

"No." She wanted to get off the phone immediately.

"Do you want me to pick you up?"

"Not . . . no. I have the car."

"You shouldn't be alone."

"I'm all right."

Evelyn held the phone tight and didn't know what to say next.

"Well, you have other people to call, I'm sure, I don't want to keep you."

"Yes."

"Should I come? Come now?"

"No. It's fine."

"You know you can always . . ."

Before Evelyn could say more, Meryl had hung up.

Meryl walked into the small bathroom near the back of the room.

She sat on the tiled floor and wrapped her arms around herself. She turned her head toward the dirty ceiling, waiting for some answer, some feeling of reassurance. But there was none.

She lay down on the floor and pressed her face against the cool tile.

Then silence came.

It struck Meryl that she would never have to sit in that hospital bathroom ever again. She had no reason to go to the hospital anymore. Tomorrow she would wake up and have nowhere she had to go.

For the smallest moment, she felt liberated.

It was terrifying.

"You always make me talk about myself, Meryl. You're very good at that."

"I do? I'm sorry, I didn't even notice."

Meryl was lying. She did notice. She did that on purpose.

"Yes, you do. I'm not talking anymore. You talk."

"What do you want to know?" It was their third date.

"Everything."

"Really?"

"Yes."

"I don't know what you want me to say. What should I say?"

"Whatever you want to."

Meryl laughed and then turned her head toward the window in the restaurant.

Was it a restaurant? She had remembered the conversation so

vividly for all of these years but couldn't place where it had happened. She just remembered the look on his face.

She closed her eyes and cradled her head in her hands. She tried to find her way into that restaurant. She could only see his face.

"I'm not joking, Meryl."

"You're sweet, Joe."

"I really want to know."

She laughed again, but Joe didn't laugh; he just stared at her. She turned her head and looked back at him once more. The smile fell off her face.

"I never think there is anything to say."

"And you just leave it at that?"

"I just can't imagine anyone really being that, I don't know, interested. So it's better that, it's better I just listen. People will be let down."

"How do you know that?"

Joe didn't laugh. He just looked at her like he understood. He reached across the table to take her hand. She could still feel the warmth of him.

"I just do."

"No."

"How do you know people won't be let down?"

And then his face turned away from her, as if he was really considering what he asked.

"I just do."

Meryl had always believed that falling in love took time, and that people grew on you, that things built slowly, and one day a decision was made to love. But real love is not made of logic or reason, and like most things of consequence, it can happen in seconds.

The day after Joe died, on the Monday, Meryl had an appointment with the funeral home director.

Five minutes late, Meryl sat down in an uncomfortable chair across from Mr. Leavitt. He was middle-aged and ruddy-faced. He was so short that she didn't trust him. He looked like a drinker, which made Meryl feel even more ill at ease.

She wanted to leave.

Mr. Leavitt adjusted himself in his chair. He cleared his throat for the tenth time.

"So we just have the final details to go over here."

"Right."

"You brought the obituary with you?"

"Yes, here."

Meryl went into her purse and brought out the obituary that Joe had written before he died.

"Okay, great. Well, it looks like everything was pre-planned here."

"Yes. I think it was."

"Did you bring what you want him to be buried in?"

"Excuse me?"

"A suit or something?"

"Oh, no. No. I completely . . . I forgot."

"That's all right. Maybe you could have someone bring it over."

"No, I'll bring it . . . this afternoon."

Mr. Leavitt nodded and looked at her without any pity. Everything was so unsentimental in his office. Maybe she liked him more than she originally thought.

"Okay. So music is picked, the time is set . . . yes. Everything here should be in order. Do you have any children that might want to look over these details?"

"We didn't have children."

"Oh, all right." Mr. Leavitt pushed himself back in his chair. In his drawer he found the bent brochure he was looking for and handed it to Meryl.

"Oftentimes people in your position find this helpful."

Meryl looked down at the brochure entitled "You Are Here: Living with Grief."

She placed the brochure on Mr. Leavitt's desk and slid it back toward him, across the shiny wooden surface.

"I wrote this."

Under different circumstances, this would probably be funny, Meryl thought. Mr. Leavitt stared at her, still short, still fat.

"No, really. I did. Meryl Johnson, that's me."

He looked down at the brochure, and there was her name in black on white. He looked back up at her, unsure what to say next.

"Do you want it, anyway?"

"No."

As Meryl left the funeral home, she wondered how she could feel so unprepared. How death could feel so absolutely different when it happened to her.

"Meryl, it's Joan. I just heard from Evelyn about Joe. I just wanted to call you and—I just wanted to tell you how sorry I am. I know, ah, I know we haven't spoken so much lately, I thought, I don't know, I thought it would be best to . . . I wanted to call. I can't imagine how difficult this is. Frank and I, well, ah, if you wouldn't mind, Frank and I would like to drop off dinner for you tonight. Would that be okay? You don't need to call back, I'll just come by and leave it, well, I guess I'll just leave it on your porch. And listen, if there is anything that you need, you know, anything at all, you just call here, okay? Well, I guess, I just wanted, I . . . Meryl, I'm so sorry. You just call if you need anything, okay?"

There were so many phone calls after the news spread, many that surprised Meryl, many that came from people she hadn't heard from in months.

When he first got sick, people came in droves. They were all so willing to give advice, to tell them it would be okay. Like every great tragedy, this one's first act was crowded with supporting players. But then, when he got sicker, the court jesters and kinsmen silently slipped away, without phone calls and without visits. As the curtain fell, only Meryl and Joe were left standing.

People scatter like cockroaches in the light when death gets too close. Anyone will come to your funeral. Not everyone will sit with you when you're on the way out.

So Meryl didn't remember having many long conversations with old friends. She remembered the absence. The loneliness.

She had come to realize that death and dying are silent.

It wasn't that she couldn't have children, it was that she didn't want them, and with no regret.

Until he got sick.

"Goddammit, Meryl, I don't need your help with this."

Joe was carrying in boxes of junk from the garage. It was six months after his diagnosis, and he had just started serious treatment. Nothing was certain yet.

"Joe, put the boxes down. They're too heavy for you."

"Shut up, Meryl, would you? I've carried boxes my whole life."

"Why are you taking all the boxes out of the garage right now?"

"Because, Meryl, all this junk needs to be dealt with. If I leave this up to you it'll never get done."

"I don't want you hurting yourself, Joe."

"Oh, Jesus Christ, Meryl! Leave me alone."

He looked at her, out of breath. He was livid, but in his eyes, Meryl knew he was pleading with her to let him pretend things were fine. Meryl could tell the box was too much for him now. He was struggling to carry it.

"Joe, stop right now. Dr. Stein said—"

"I don't give a fuck, Meryl—"

"Joe! Keep your voice down, the neighbours . . ."

"I don't give a fuck about them either. Don't touch this box."

"Joe! I'm only trying to help you! Put the box down," she said, trying to take the boxes from him.

"Meryl, for the last time, I don't need your fucking help!" And with that he yanked the box out of Meryl's hands, causing her to stumble backward.

Meryl watched him getting smaller and smaller as he walked up their driveway. In all the years they were married he had never been as mean to her as he was after he got sick. He would break his back if it meant not acknowledging the reality of what was going on. He didn't need to be looking at old pictures and tools and records, everything they had accumulated over the decades. He needed to be resting. He needed to be fighting. He was so stupid when he wanted to be.

Meryl waited a good five minutes to go inside. Then, slowly, she walked up their long gravel driveway. If he's going to act like this, he can make his own dinner, she thought as she walked in the front door. She was going to walk right past him, say nothing, and spend the night in their bedroom reading.

But when she walked into the living room she found Joe lying on the couch, arms at his side, staring at the ceiling. The boxes lay scattered on the floor. He'd turned the baseball game on, but he wasn't watching it. As she walked past him, he caught her eye. His face was scored with pain.

She stood and stared at him for a few seconds. Then she walked into the kitchen and brought him out his painkillers and a glass of water. He accepted.

After a few minutes, she sat next to him on the couch while the television yelled, "Swing! Batter, batter, swing!"

Meryl had just finished forcing her breakfast down when Evelyn and Larry rang her doorbell. They had offered to drive her to the service.

Meryl came to the door, dressed in a black dress that she would never, ever wear again.

"Hi," said Evelyn.

"Thanks for coming," said Meryl.

"Of course," said Larry.

They stood in the doorway. They seemed nervous. Meryl didn't know if she should invite them in.

"So it's ten-thirty, sorry we're a little late. Do you think maybe we should get in the car now?" asked Evelyn.

"Oh, yes, sure. Let me just get my purse."

"Oh, Meryl?" interrupted Larry.

"Yes?"

"You . . . have a little jam on your face."

"Oh." Meryl raised her hand to face and wiped the left side of her mouth.

"The other side."

She quickly turned around to find her purse and wiped the right side of her mouth, embarrassed.

Evelyn moved closer to Larry when Meryl's back was turned. She forced her face to his. Her eyes widened and her lips spread tightly across her teeth, concerned. When Meryl turned around they jumped apart, and Evelyn smiled to cover the sudden movement. Larry quickly whispered something to her. While he was in her ear, Evelyn looked Meryl up and down, nodding in agreement.

"Wait, Meryl, do you think, you maybe want to have a drink before we go?"

"At this hour?"

"Well, I was just thinking, if you wanted to. We could. Only if you wanted, though."

"No, no, I don't."

"Okay."

Larry looked around.

"So, we should maybe hit the road then," he said.

"Yeah, we should," agreed Evelyn.

Meryl nodded and looked around her living room one last time. Turning back toward the door, she caught her reflection in the mirror. She was shaking like a leaf. She hadn't noticed.

"Will you two just excuse me for a second? I'm a little chilly, I think I'll go get a shawl."

Meryl went upstairs but not to her closet. She went to her bathroom. She opened the medicine cabinet and took two of the tranquillizers that Dr. Stein had prescribed, against her will, months ago when she told him she had trouble sleeping. She threw some water on her face and looked at herself in the mirror once more. She took measured breaths and tried to make her trembling stop.

A few minutes later, she came down her stairs.

"Meryl, where's your shawl?" asked Evelyn.

"Oh . . . I couldn't find it," Meryl said, a little more slowly than she should have.

Meryl had only been drunk once in her life. It was very late at night, decades ago. She had found an old bottle of gin that Joe had got as a present from some colleague. It burned her throat as it went down.

She sat in her dim kitchen, with her bare feet against the linoleum tile, drinking. Her elbows were pressed hard on her cold plastic table. Her wrists supported her tired face. She was half dressed. That night she let her newly soft stomach stick out and sag. Joe was sleeping in a motel twenty miles east.

"Meryl, it was a slip. It was a mistake," he had told her.

That's how he described it to her. A "slip" with the woman down the street.

As the alcohol moved through her, she asked herself what she had missed. How this could have happened. What she had done wrong.

She got up and staggered across the kitchen to get a glass of water. She hadn't realized how drunk she was until she stood up. Everything around her blurred, she couldn't feel her feet. Then, without noticing until she was on the floor, she slipped on the new tile. She hit her shoulder on the way down.

"Joe!" she yelled out when the pain came a few seconds later. Then she remembered he wasn't there.

She picked herself up, like a child learning how to walk, and went to her telephone. She asked her operator to dial the number of the motel. She was transferred to his room.

"J-Joe. Joe. Come home. Please come home."

"Meryl, are you all right?"

"No . . . no. Come home now."

Before he came in the front door, Meryl steadied herself against the banister as she made her way up the stairs to their bedroom. The pictures of them on the wall spun next to her. She went to their bed and didn't get under the covers. She fell asleep immediately and didn't stir.

She woke up nauseous, but next to Joe, just like every morning for as long as she could remember.

Meryl walked into the red-brick funeral home with Larry and Evelyn.

They were greeted by a blond girl with tight ringlets. She looked sixteen.

"Hi! My name is Anna. Who is Mrs. Johnson?"

Meryl raised her hand. She didn't know why she did that. It wasn't school. But she stood still with left her hand suspended in the air. Evelyn noticed and guided her hand back down.

"I'm very sorry for your loss, Mrs. Johnson. Mr. Leavitt told me everything, so everything is in order for today. We have a room, downstairs, in the basement if you'd like to go sit there for some privacy. For you and family."

"Can these two come?" asked Meryl.

Anna looked back and forth between Evelyn and Larry.

"Yes, certainly. I'll show you where it is."

As Anna walked them down the hall and then down the stairs, Meryl noticed a lot of posters on the wall. Posters of Jesus, posters of Mary, posters of God. They were all sepia or black and white, too much grey. Everywhere she looked, the eyes on the posters followed her.

After Anna left them in the small, windowless room, Meryl turned to Evelyn. "Such serious pictures everywhere, don't you think?"

Looking around the room at all the religious artefacts, Evelyn nodded and said, "Well, no one's laughing at God in a funeral home."

And with that, Evelyn, Larry, and Meryl sat in the three armchairs provided. Meryl crossed her legs, and no one spoke. She remembered how at the few funerals she attended for the people she worked with, she told the families the person was watching everything unfold from a better place. Meryl wondered if Joe was watching right now.

Was he laughing?

It was late, and Meryl and Joe lay in bed together. They had just got the test results. It didn't look good.

Meryl rested her head on Joe's chest. She felt herself rise with every inhale and fall with every exhale. The wind whipped their window, creating an erratic tapping noise. They both knew the other wasn't asleep.

"What are we going to do, my darling?"

Meryl raised herself up and looked at his face. For the first time in a long time he was without the confident mask he wore for her.

"Well . . . we are going to fight," she said.

"What if I don't win?"

"You will win."

"But what if I don't, Meryl? I don't know if, I'm so tired."

"You will," she said louder than she wanted.

"What if I don't?"

"You will. You and I will. Together, Joe. You are going to beat this, remember?"

He went quiet for a moment. Then, almost silently, he whispered, "I don't know."

Meryl was so angry.

"You can't think like that. You know at work I always say, and I mean it, Staying present is an important part of staying functional, of beating this. We have to think about right now, not what might happen."

"I don't know," he said once more.

"No, Joe. You have to believe that you can do it. And you have to talk about it. We have to talk about it. We have to own it."

He looked at her like he didn't have the strength to keep talking.

"You can't give up. I always say that you have to believe you can beat it. You have to believe it."

"What if that's all just bullshit?"

She felt the tears burn her eyes. She turned away and lay on her side, her back to him.

"It's not."

"Okay."

The tapping continued at the window. The space that separated their bodies lay between them. Meryl wouldn't move. She didn't want him to know she was crying like that. She watched the clock tick, and twenty minutes passed where they didn't say anything.

Then, once more, he asked, "What are we going to do, my darling?"

Then she turned to him and lay her head back on his chest. He would feel the wetness of her tears on his bare chest. He moved his hand back and forth on her shoulder.

"It'll be okay," he promised.

The funeral home was almost full. Halfway through, Meryl looked around and saw a lot of faces she didn't recognize. She put her hand on Evelyn's hand and held it tight.

"Who are those people to the left and two rows back?" Meryl whispered.

Then the minister spoke loudly, drawing her back into service.

"Joe, knowing the nature of his illness, asked to write his own obituary. He also asked that it be read at his funeral. I am going to now share it with all of you, his friends and loved ones. Joe Johnson was born on April 18, 1942, just outside of Delaware. He died on August 4, 2008, just outside of Baltimore, Maryland. He was sixty-six years old.

"Joe attended teachers' college at the University of Syracuse, New York. Upon his graduation in 1964, he returned home to Delaware for what he thought would be a drunk and debauched two weeks before heading to Europe to 'find himself.' Little did he know that on his first Saturday night back he would see Meryl Vernon, the love of his life, across a dirty, smoky bar.

"Knowing immediately that she was out of his league, Joe cancelled his trip and stayed in Delaware, convinced he could trick Meryl into loving him. Somehow, he did, and a few months later, they moved to Baltimore, where he was offered a job as a history teacher. They married three years later. He remained in Baltimore for the rest of his life, and became, against his will, an avid fan of the Orioles.

"He thoroughly enjoyed his work as a teacher. He believed the kids kept him young, and no one could argue with summers off. For eighteen years he coached more than half the sports teams, and in eighteen years his baseball team, the Catonsville Bears, won ten championships. In retrospect, he realized he got lazy somewhere there in the 1980s. Upon his retirement, he continued to watch the Bears play, hollering encouraging hints from the sidelines, from 'My grandma can run faster than you!' to 'Don't worry, that ball didn't want to be caught anyway!' Five percent of his pension will be donated to the Catonsville Bears and their upkeep, so that the kids will always remember Mr. Johnson's advice, even from beyond the grave.

"Joe is survived by the far most significant and important part of his life, his wife, Meryl. She was the best thing that ever happened to him, and he went to sleep every night feeling lucky to have known her. She made him laugh, mostly at himself. She was smarter than he was, but like any good wife, sometimes she let him believe otherwise. She aged well too.

"But above all, she loved him even when he didn't deserve it. And he loved her as much on the day he died as the first moment he saw her.

"His only regret upon his passing is that they didn't get more time together.

"He thanks everyone for coming, and reminds Meryl that he is not lost. He is only waiting to be found."

It is nighttime and Meryl lies on the grass in her front yard. She can't sleep. Darkness came hours ago. She tries to count every star in the sky.

She wakes up to the newspaper boy gently shaking her, a stricken look on his face. She is still dressed in black.

"Do you want me to walk you into your house, ma'am? Do you live here?"

"I live here. I'm all right. I couldn't sleep."

"Are you sick?"

She shook her head. She straightened her dress. He helped her stand.

Meryl turns to her house. Why is it still standing?

"Is this your house?"

Meryl put her fingertips on his lips. Why did everyone act as if they were the same person as yesterday?

Gun Shy

His fist collides with face, his knuckles cutting through his opponent's soft cheeks, knifing deeper and deeper through his flesh, against his pointed teeth. He feels the boy's jaw separate and move farther to the side than it should.

The boy doesn't make a sound.

He feels a hit right under his chin, forcing his bottom teeth against the roof of his mouth. He spits blood.

He kicks the boy square in the guts. He feels his foot stopped against sinewy stomach. The kick lands more softly than he had hoped. He draws his foot backward again, kicking the boy again.

The boy falls to the ground, scraping his body against the pavement, the kick leaving a lasting impression. He's winded, howling for air.

Michael reaches down and gives him a hand.

"Thanks, Mike." He spits.

"You done?"

"Yeah." Loveday, the boy, nods.

Mike helps him off the ground.

"You bleeding?" he asks.

"Nah, not really. You?"

"Just a little," he says, pointing to his mouth. "Nothing serious."

Mike and Loveday started their fight club not long after they met. It's only the two of them. Not exclusive, really, but no one else is all that into it.

"Fuck, that was hard," says Loveday.

"That's what your mom said."

Loveday laughs and so does Michael, until he realizes that it's not that funny when you're actually fucking the guy's mom.

Holding ice to his lip, Michael stands in his messy bedroom.

His clothes are always too baggy and he's always overdressed, wearing a suit jacket or tie, sometimes both. He likes it that way, telling Loveday's mom, Lauren, that "it's glamorous to be dressed up with nowhere to go."

This morning he stands, still with nowhere to go, in front of his mirror for a little longer than usual. The mirror is plastered with pictures of Bob Dylan, guitars, and ghetto superstars.

Michael is tall and skinny and good-looking, even if he doesn't think so. He has a thoughtful face, the type that becomes more handsome with age.

"You will look good weathered," she told him after she swept her fingertips across his face, before she kissed him for the first time. His face is young, which Michael hates, but that's what she's fallen in love with. The youngness brings her closer to what she could have had.

His cheeks and chin are sprinkled with the hopeful stubble that only sixteen-year-old boys grow. All together, his features portray an acute sensitivity. Michael was the little boy that other boys picked on because he looked soft, and so, he also hates his sensitivity. But the sensitivity is remarkable and apparent, and no matter how he tries to mask it, it remains.

"You have no idea how arresting you are," she said last night after they made love.

"My Bob Dylan," she calls him.

He angles his face and juts his jaw out toward the mirror. His face looks thinnest that way. He takes off his shirt and throws it on the floor with the other mess. He looks back up to the mirror. He sees the angles of his body. His concave chest. His protruding lower stomach. It's the only souvenir he has left to remind him he used to be the fat kid that everyone hated. He stares at the extra flesh. He grabs all of it.

"Fuck."

He sucks in his gut and turns to the side. He decides he looks better from the side. Taller, thinner, a little more like Dylan.

"You have a beautiful body," she told him last night, her sweaty hands moving along his broad back, before he entered her.

He smiles.

Then Michael is struck by a thought that is as uplifting as it is crushing. Looking in the mirror this morning was the longest time in his memory when he wasn't thinking about numbers or doing math in his head. It's uplifting because Michael hates thinking about math, even though he sees numbers everywhere he looks. It's crushing because, now that he's noticed, he's thinking about numbers again. The only time he doesn't think about them is when he's fighting, fucking, or high. Consequently, he tries to participate in those three activities as often as humanly possible.

"Mike! Hurry up! You're going to miss your bus."

"Ma, relax!"

He's thinking about prime numbers now. 2, 3, 5, 7, 11, 13, 17, 19.

Michael has a special relationship with numbers. He doesn't see them, he feels them, as shapes and colours. Seven is blue, rectangular, kind of scary. Three is red, circular, pretty relaxed. Ten is yellow, star-shaped, overwhelming. He likes four the best because it's purple and reminds him of his old friend Caitlin.

He grabs a blue button-up shirt from the floor. He throws it on and decides he likes it. It makes him look sophisticated.

He runs out of his room and then down the stairs, counting every step.

He meets his mother as he's trying to get out the front door.

"Did you eat breakfast?" she asks.

"No, I'm going to be late."

"You are going to make yourself sick if you don't start eating more."

"Sure, Ma."

He grabs his Dodgers cap and checks his reflection in the glass panel of the front door. He tells himself he looks "fresh" and "ill," his two favourite adjectives. He throws his ears in and grabs his Ray-Bans. It's too dark for sunglasses, not the season, but he wears them anyway.

"Bye, Ma."

And he's out the door.

"You're not crazy, honey. You're autistic. It's different."

That's what his mom would tell him when he was a kid, and he'd come home crying because he couldn't keep the numbers away, convinced he was a lunatic and that nothing could be done to fix him.

"Bill Gates is autistic," he told Lauren a few weeks after they started fucking. Meaning, he's not retarded, but that he has some extraordinary abilities that leave him feeling extraordinarily disabled as a result.

"So, what are you?" she asked. "A genius?"

"Yeah. I'm a useless fucking genius."

He's gifted, but there's still nothing that can be done to fix him.

He gets on the bus.

He feels around in his pocket. He only has a roach and five dollars on him.

"Fuck."

Now there's no way he can get high until school's out, and that's if he's lucky. Hopefully, someone will smoke him on some between classes because he's broke as a joke right now. He tells himself that he shouldn't have smoked that extra spliff before bed last night, but he just couldn't get to sleep after sneaking home from Lauren.

"I love you," she'd told him for the first time ever.

He didn't say it back. Should he have?

He nods at the bus driver, a familiar face, as he pays his fare. He looks around the bus. None of his friends are on yet.

"Gay."

He's disappointed because with no other option, dumb chit-chat distracts him. When he's distracted, the numbers disappear, sometimes for up to a minute.

He turns his iPod up, and a Jay Dee remix comes on. There's a lot of instrumental, which makes counting the beats hard. He bobs his head up and down to the music, trying to shake the numbers out.

But he can't.

He changes the song. It's Dylan's "Up to Me." He turns it up even louder. He breathes deep and feels a little better.

Today is going to be a long fucking day, he thinks.

When Michael gets off the bus, he has to walk a block before he gets to school. There are a lot of cars parked up and down the street. He adds up all the numbers on their licence plates. When he feels the final answer, he always feels it in his left arm.

"Go away. Just go away. I don't want you today," he says, hitting his left arm, hard. It doesn't work, and he hopes none of the other kids walking to school noticed him talking to himself.

Why is it so bad this morning? He was doing way better with numbers, thinking about them less, especially since Lauren. But it's bad today, the worst it's been in a long time.

"Motherfucker."

He gets to the front doors of the school, looks at his watch.

8:55. Five minutes before class.

Eight plus five is thirteen. Thirteen times eight is one hundred and four. One hundred and four divided by fifty-five is one point eight nine zero nine zero.

He's thankful he has math class first period. At least that gives him a reason to be thinking about all these numbers. Maybe he can relax a bit. He lights a smoke. Halfway through his cigarette, Loveday approaches him. Mike was just thinking about Lauren's wet pussy, but he tries to act normal.

Michael and Loveday have a complicated relationship. When Mike was fat, Loveday was athletic and popular. He ruined Mike's life. Mike sometimes thinks that's why he's fucking his mom—to get him back. But then lately, all these feelings have come up, and he can't be sure that anything is true anymore.

About eighteen months ago, when Mike lost all the weight (thanks, cigarettes), he started smoking weed behind the school where Loveday and all his friends smoked. It was bizarre at first; Michael was constantly plagued by that vulnerable feeling you get when you stick your arm out of a moving car and everything inside you wants you to put it back. But he persevered, mysteriously stoic, and Loveday had matured, slightly. After a few weeks of silent avoidance, they started burning joints together.

They've been friends ever since. Now Mike is considered athletic and popular, which is all he ever wanted for as long as he can remember. Sometimes he wakes up in the middle of the night, breathless and confused, lost in all the change, still trying to convince himself that things really are different now. Then he puts his hand on his heart and counts the racing beats until he falls back asleep.

Sometimes, when Mike is too high, when he's at their house for dinner, when they're just chilling, he thinks Loveday can see how he destroyed him. And then sometimes, when Loveday is too high, he remembers everything he's said and done. But they don't get too high very often.

And they never talk about it.

In the past couple of weeks, Mike decided that their being friends is more difficult for Loveday than it is for him. Well, minus the whole mom thing.

"What's up, buddy?" says Loveday.

"Nothing, can I grab off you?" Mike asks.

"No, man. Sorry, I smoked my last spliff just now."

"Shit, eh?"

"Yeah, sorry. How's your lip?"

"Iced it. It's fine."

"So, tomorrow. Same time?"

"Sure."

Michael notices that Loveday is wearing a Leonard Cohen shirt. He points at it.

"'You don't really care for music, do you?'"

"Huh?"

"'You don't really care for music, do you?'" Mike says and almost sings so that Loveday will get the joke.

"Nah, man, I love music. I fucking play the guitar."

"Oh, no, that's a Cohen line. From 'Hallelujah'?"

"Oh yeah? That song's sick, eh?"

They stand together. They don't talk.

The sky is grey above them, and it smells like rain. Mike feels all the angles in the negative space of the field just due north.

Obtuse from the goalpost to the bleachers. Green and angry. Ninety degrees from the trees to the diamond. Pink and soft. One hundred and eighty from the basketball net to the ground. Blue and sad.

Then the bell rings.

"Shit, man. We got math," says Loveday.

"Yeah, I know."

And Mike and Loveday walk the halls, giving props to all the boys they pass. Mike climbs the stairs, faster than Loveday, counting every step, feeling it, all the way up.

"Sweetheart, you have this opportunity to go to a better high school because of your math scores. Why won't you take it?"

"Because fuck it, Ma."

"Fuck it isn't an answer."

"I hate math."

"No, you don't."

"Yes, I do."

"How?"

"Because I see numbers like you hear jet planes." Her face looked like glass and it broke his heart to watch it shatter.

When he walks into math class, Michael notices his old friend Caitlin already sitting at her desk. He smiles at her. She notices and doesn't smile back. Caitlin is blond and thin, delicately beautiful. Or at least Mike thinks so.

They haven't spoken in about eight months. They used to be best friends. Caitlin was one of the only people who was nice to Michael when he was fat. They played video games and listened to music and talked about math. Caitlin thought he was really funny. That made him feel really good.

They stopped speaking a little after he lost the weight. Mike says it was because they grew apart, but it was really because she didn't like his new friends. The boys don't like her either.

"She's a flat, uptight bitch."

They would probably put up with the uptight bitch part, but it's the flat-chested thing they really can't get past. Mike doesn't laugh when they say it, but he doesn't stop them either.

He's angry with her. He wishes he and Caitlin still talked, that they could be how they were. Sometimes he chats with her on the Internet, but it gets pretty heavy, so he doesn't start up conversations too often.

She doesn't reply most of the time anyway.

The math teacher, Mr. Trin, an Asian guy who can hardly speak English, walks into the class.

"Okay, kid, we have test back here."

The kids groan; the test was hard. Mike groans too, but for no reason. He got perfect. He always does.

Mr. Trin moves up and down the aisles of desks. When he hands Mike his test, Mike sees the red 100% with a circle around it. He immediately stuffs it into his bag.

Mike's red-haired friend Travis, who they all call Fire Crotch, turns to him.

"Fuck, man. I failed again! How'd you do?"

"Yeah, me too," says Mike.

Caitlin looks at him when he says it. He moves his eyes away from her. Fire Crotch keeps talking.

"That test was so gay."

"So gay."

Mr. Trin turns to Michael.

"Michael, what you say test was?"

"I said the test was gay, sir."

The whole class laughs a little.

"What you say?"

"I said the test was gay." Mike speaks extra slow, just so Mr. Trin can really hear him.

By this point all the guys in the class are laughing and most of the girls too. Fire Crotch has tears in his eyes.

When Michael sees how lost Mr. Trin looks, he thinks he might have gone too far. He tells himself he wouldn't have said that if he'd gotten high enough this morning. Shit just gets so aggravating when he's too sober.

Caitlin looks at her textbook, stone-faced. Mike notices and feels like an idiot for a split second.

"Michael, you go to office. Now!" says Mr. Trin.

"Nah."

The whole class has erupted by now. Some kids are laughing, others are just taking the opportunity to talk and not do math. Mr. Trin looks even more lost. Then, just loud enough so everyone can hear, Caitlin looks at Michael and says, "Michael, can you fuck off?"

"Bitch," says Fire Crotch, still laughing.

"Leave her alone," says Mike. He feels so sick whenever they're mean to her.

"What are you? Fucking her?" asks Fire Crotch, disgusted.

"I said leave her alone," says Mike. He's not kidding. Fire Crotch is going to get punched.

"Jesus, chill," says Fire Crotch. He wipes his eyes and stops laughing.

"Caitlin, you go to office too. No swearing," says Mr. Trin, scrambling to keep order. His voice is much louder than it needs to be.

Caitlin looks at Mr. Trin. She's too dignified to show how upset she is. She gets her books together and heads to the office.

Mike follows her.

Caitlin walks down the hall very quickly, not wanting Mike to catch up to her. He calls after her.

"Caitlin, I'm sorry about them. They're assholes."

The few stragglers in the hall look at him like he's crazy, whispering to each other. Caitlin moves fast, and Mike is counting her every step. It gets hard to keep counting with her practically running. He's anxious, he doesn't like being distracted by the counting.

"Just talk to me."

Suddenly the counting is overpowered by the *clip-clop* sound her shoes make on the floor.

It's a sound that makes Mike hurt. He used to hear that sound on their walk home every day. Now, he can't remember the last time he heard it.

"Caitlin, please. I'm sorry. They're stupid."

She keeps walking. He starts counting again. He feels fours all over his left arm.

"Caitlin, please. Turn around. I'm sorry."

She stops. He stops counting. The fours go away.

"What do you want, Mike?"

"Nothing. I'm sorry. I was being a retard. It's all my fault that happened."

He hasn't seen her face this close in a long time. It's thinner than it used to be. It's more delicate. Her eyes look greener. He counts the freckles on her face. Thirty-three. Thirty-four including the one on her lip. She must have gotten some sun because there are more than usual. Usually there are twenty-one. Twenty-two, including the one on her lip.

He wonders if she can tell that's what he's doing. She used to always be able to tell when he was counting her freckles. She would tell him to stop, that her freckles embarrassed her. But he knew she secretly liked it, that it made her feel special.

"What do you want, Mike?"

"Nothing."

She turns away from him and continues walking down the hall even faster. His counting gets really speedy and all-consuming.

One step. Two steps. Three steps. Four, five, six, seven, eight, nine, ten, eleven, twelve, thirteen.

Then she stops for a moment.

He stops counting.

"I hope you're happy," she says.

She starts walking again, and he keeps counting but doesn't follow her.

He stands in the hall, watching her get smaller and smaller in the distance. He misses her. So much. That's all he was trying to say.

In thirty-six more steps, she's turned a corner to the office. The *clip-clopping* ends. Once everything stops, he can think again.

He decides he's not going to the principal's office. Fuck that, he thinks. He wants to go home. This day is already shitty and it's only going to get shittier.

In the parking lot on his way out, he runs into his friend Dave. Dave smokes him on a joint. Real charitable of him. After a few hits, Mike gives Dave props and leaves.

Then he thinks about something he wishes he hadn't. Dave would have never smoked him if he was the way he used to be. He hates thinking about stuff like that, and usually can push those thoughts away, but today he can't.

Why is it so hard today?

Wu-Tang plays in his ears. He thinks he needs to go home and take a nap.

Then he thinks, Man, nothing is how it used to be.

And before he can stop himself, he remembers how things used to be.

Mike walks into math class. He walked much slower then, when he was heavier. It would take him sixty-three steps to get from his locker to the class. It takes him thirty-five now, thirty-two on a good day. He looks at the ground and doesn't make eye contact with anyone until he sees Caitlin. He smiles a lot when he sees her, and she smiles a lot back.

There's a spare desk next to her. Thank God, he thinks. He hates having to sit next to most of the guys in his class. They don't like sitting next to him either.

"Hey, buddy," says Caitlin.

"Hey. How's your day?"

Before she can answer, Loveday walks into the class. Mike feels his heart beat a little faster. About two and a half times in two seconds. He looks down. He doesn't want to catch Loveday's eye.

Mr. Norad starts speaking. He taught math in ninth grade. He was a pretty nice teacher except he asked Mike to write the answers on the board too often. Mike didn't like the attention. Hated it, actually.

"Okay, who did the homework last night?" asks Mr. Norad.

Caitlin raises her hand and looks expectantly at Mike. He doesn't want to raise his hand, but he does for her.

"Of course those two did."

"That's enough, Brian," says Mr. Norad. "Now, did anyone have trouble with number six?"

Most of the kids in the class nod.

"Mike, would you like to come up and write it out for us?" asks Mr. Norad, smiling and encouraging.

Mike's stomach falls. He has a bad feeling, wants to avoid drawing attention to himself as much as possible.

"No, that's okay,"

But when Mike says okay, his voice cracks. His voice cracked a lot then.

"Ha! Did you hear that? What's wrong with your voice, faggot?"

"Nothing." But his voice cracks again.

Loveday laughs even harder. "Ha! You did it again!"

"More than enough, Brian," says Mr. Norad. "If this continues, you will leave."

Mike's face turns even redder. They were all talking so quickly, and he couldn't keep up.

"Why is your face red, faggot?" another voice yells.

"Enough!" says Mr. Norad again.

Mike feels exceedingly flustered and alone. He can tell his face is getting really red. He is sweating a lot. He turns around to Loveday.

"I don't, I don't have a . . ." but before he can finish, his voice cracks again. His voice always cracks when he is nervous. He turns and swears at himself silently for saying anything at all.

"Look! His voice cracked again. He's nervous! He likes you, Loveday."

"Don't even look at me, fat ass."

"That's it, Brian! Get out!" screams Mr. Norad.

Everyone in the class is laughing.

Mike buries his face in his textbook.

"Why is he putting his face in his book like that?" he hears one girl from the back of his class say.

No one will stop laughing.

"If I hear another word from any of you, I swear the whole lot of you are getting detention. Silence right now," Mr. Norad says.

Then Mike feels Caitlin's small hand on his knee. She squeezes his knee, harder than usual, because she knows he gets forgetful during times like this. She really wants him to feel it. He turns and looks at her. He can tell his face looks really worried because of her reaction.

"Don't worry about them," she whispers. "Just don't say anything. They're assholes."

"What was that, Caitlin?" asks Mr. Norad.

"I said they're assholes."

Mr. Norad looks at her. He doesn't say anything else.

A silence falls over the class. Mike guesses no one else wants detention.

Mr. Norad turns back to Mike and looks at him, encouraging.

"Now, Michael, if you would please answer question six on the board."

Getting up in front of the class is the last thing Mike wants to do. But he can't open his mouth and say no again because he knows his voice will crack. Why is he always so emotional?

He gets up out of his desk, looks at the floor, and walks ten measured steps to the board. He picks up the white chalk and starts writing the equations on the board.

He feels the answers all over his left arm. He feels blues, yellows, greens, purples, oranges. The humiliation falls away. All he can feel is the numbers. The anger of the numbers, the joy of the numbers, the sadness of the numbers. They blend, then fall apart, and before he knows it, he isn't thinking anymore. He is just writing and feeling. Writing and feeling. Writing and feeling.

The truth is that he never liked math. It never made him happy, but he needed it then. It made them quiet.

It carried him far, far away.

When Mike gets home he's beat. On his walk home he did the licence plates again. The weed helped a little, but he couldn't really stop himself. He multiplied them, divided them, added them, subtracted them, without thinking.

He has a headache now. He knew he would. With every new feeling in his left arm, he told them he hated them. He didn't need them, not anymore. He just wanted them to go away.

But they wouldn't.

He eats a ham sandwich, barefoot in his kitchen. As soon as he finishes, he heads up the stairs and goes to bed.

Lying in bed, almost asleep, he wonders to himself if his left arm would fall asleep even after he has. He doesn't want to dream of numbers.

The last thing he remembers thinking about is Caitlin.

Caitlin and her pretty freckles.

Caitlin and her green eyes.

Caitlin and her sad face.

He feels fours.

Michael dreams of tall buildings.

He dreams of tall trees.

He dreams of tall ladders.

He falls, far, far down.

When he lands, he sees women dressed up like the olden days. They have big skirts and fancy hats. He can't see their faces because they are veiled in lace. He asks the women to show him their faces, but they won't. He thinks one of the women is Caitlin, or an old relative of Caitlin, but he can't be certain because she won't show him her face. The lady walks like Caitlin, but when he taps her on the shoulder, she won't turn around.

He stops by a river and watches an old man paint a picture of the scenery. The painting looks like a perfect photograph. Everything looks exactly the same as what's in front of him. Michael can't believe anyone can paint like that. When he goes to compliment the artist, the man won't turn around.

After a few tries, Michael decides he should leave the river. He walks down a dusty road. He sees people on horses, men in carriages, women in petticoats.

Then he falls again.

He falls far, far down and lands nowhere he's even been before.

He doesn't see numbers.

Just tall buildings.

Tall trees.

Tall ladders.

In a moment of lucidity, he tells himself to keep dreaming.

Michael wakes up to his phone buzzing.

Fire Crotch texted him: dude whered u go? meet at licks. now. peace.

Licks is a diner three blocks from Michael's house. He looks at the clock on his phone. It's five-thirty.

Five plus three is eight. Five times three is fifteen. Fifteen divided by eight is one point eight seven five. One point eight seven five divided by eight times three is zero point seven zero three one two five.

He can't believe he's slept that long. He rolls onto his back. His left arm really hurts, but his headache's gone. His insides feel empty.

He throws on his jeans. Looking in his mirror, he decides he looks better in the evening light. He checks his pockets, and he still has the five dollars from earlier.

He still has the roach too.

The boys will probably smoke him on something, he thinks.

He runs down the stairs and counts every step. He doesn't see his mom. She's still at work. He throws his earphones in, and this time the Geto Boys come on.

Two beats.

Four beats.

Eight beats.

Sixteen beats.

When Michael gets to the diner the boys are already seated in the corner booth. He is met by the cute waitress, a year older than them and it really shows. The uniform hugs every part of her, and when she asks if she can get anything started for him, Michael looks at his Air Forces.

He tells the pretty girl that he'd like a grilled cheese and a Coke. Then he thanks her.

"No problem," she says, smiling as she walks away.

He walks toward the boys. Seeing all them, Fire Crotch, Loveday, the others, still makes him nervous. The reaction is instantaneous; his hurting stomach, the cold sweating.

He tells himself to relax, that things are different now. He reminds himself that they are friends. Things are different.

He swallows, tells his face not to look nervous. He adjusts his jaw and puts a vacancy in his eyes. He tries to look tough, like the rappers, and walks toward them with his chest out. He walks slower than usual.

"What's up?" he says as he slides into the booth.

"Nothing, man, where the fuck did you go earlier?" asks Loveday.

"Yeah, did you go to the principal's office?" says Fire Crotch.

"Fuck that. I went home."

"Sweet, man," says Loveday, smiling and proud. "Fucking Caitlin came back like halfway through class."

"Oh, yeah?" says Mike.

"Yeah, her face was like beet red. She looked like she'd been crying. She's such a bitch. She'd probably kill herself if she got in trouble."

"Shut up," says Michael quietly.

"Whatever, she's a bitch. That waitress is so fit, eh?"

Michael turns and looks at her. This time he really looks at her.

"Yeah," he says.

She is beautiful, Michael decides. She has a soft face, soft curves, long curly blond hair. She looks angelic and special.

He thinks that she must have come from a family that really loves her. She looks like she respects herself. He bets she works really hard at this job. She probably has it for a reason. Maybe she's paying for college. Or maybe she has a dad who can't work, so she got a job to help.

Michael thinks about how he would like to talk to her. How he'd like to count her freckles. How he'd like to see what she thinks about working at Licks. How maybe they could be friends, like he and Caitlin were. Then maybe he could take her out for dinners. They could watch movies and talk about music. He thinks he could trust her. He wants to tell her about the numbers. He wants to tell her how he sees them everywhere. She looks like she would understand.

"Look at that ass," says Fire Crotch.

Michael turns and stops looking at her. He looks around the booth. His friends' faces look different under the fluorescent lights. Their faces look gnarled and wooden. When they laugh, they look like goblins or vampires with pointed teeth and shiny eyes. Michael blinks, tells himself that his eyes are playing tricks on him. But when he opens them again, everyone still looks different. The colours around him fade away, and everyone looks ghoulish and like characters in the scary movies he and Caitlin would watch. He can't recognize any of them. It makes him frightened.

He thinks maybe he smoked some bad weed, but then he remembers he didn't smoke hardly any weed today.

Eventually he has to turn away from them; he doesn't want them to think that he's looking at them strangely. But when he turns away, he can feel all the angles in the diner. He doesn't want to think about numbers so he looks back at his friends. He tries to not focus on their faces, to just listen to the conversation.

"I met my cousins last weekend. They are so fucking hot."

"You're related, you fuck."

"Not really. I'm adopted."

The pretty waitress comes back and gives everyone their bill. She looks uncomfortable, and Michael wonders if she heard what the boys were saying about her earlier. He smiles at her, and she smiles back. For a moment, he thinks she can tell he is separate from the group. That he's different. That he didn't say those things. That he never would. That he would be good to her.

But then she turns and leaves.

They all look at the bill. The total is $56.58. She didn't give them separate ones.

"Shit, what do we owe?"

"Fuck, I hate it when they don't split it up."

Michael looks at the bill and his left arm immediately hurts.

He knows what they owe.

$56.58 divided by six is $9.43.

They each owe $9.43.

But he doesn't say anything. He gets up. He finds the waitress near the door. He gives her his five. "You're a really good waitress," he says.

He walks to Lauren's house. Loveday will be home soon and he shouldn't be there.

He kisses her, determined, his tongue searching to get into her mouth.

"I love you too," he tells her.

The wet tears fall down his face and onto her dark hair.

The Way We Were

"Go," he said.

It was one of those conversations that had been happening for months, those that never really begin, those with no end in sight. He and I had moved back and forth, our bodies forced together, tangled in a weeks-long waltz with no final step.

Michael and I had been together for two years. Six years, if you count the technicalities. Growing up, he was the boy who'd take me on dates if I wanted him to, invite me to parties on the weekend. I was his first kiss. He wasn't mine. It wasn't until I turned sixteen that I decided I could love him too. I was so used to him that he was a part of me, but sometimes, when I'd look at him and I couldn't recognize his face.

"Go," he said again.

For the first time we'd both stopped moving. I was eighteen. I was leaving and I couldn't carry him with me. I knew then that the dance was done. His face was resigned, tired, plastered with loss. I'd never met a face so suited for sorrow.

"Go," he said, the last time.

I held him the way you hold someone you'll never hold again. Tightly, desperate to squeeze out of them what's left to take. He held me with just his body, two arms and one chest, bones and nothing else.

When I let go, he was buried so deep inside himself that I don't think he even saw me leave. Now, I'm buried, drinking, drunk, lost in long nights and strange men.

"Don't forget me, Grace," he said as I left.

"I won't," the voice inside my head told me.

If only I'd known I'd end up here.

It's a Tuesday night.

I can't feel my body anymore and I'm so grateful. When I can still feel my body I can still hear the voice in my head and I can't dance like this.

The Rolling Stones' "Under My Thumb" is playing on the jukebox, and it's my favourite song forever from now on. My body that I can see beneath me, but that I can't feel, is moving with a harmonized surrender.

My feet shuffle from side to side. When I lift my head toward the ceiling, I can feel that my face doesn't look how it usually does. I notice my hands floating all around. They surprise me every time because I'm not telling them to go anywhere. They just move.

Everyone I know thinks I'm a good dancer, but I'm not. I'm just a good performer and I've always been very good at faking. Before this summer when I'd dance, I was moving how I thought I should, how other people wanted to see me.

I told those liquid sounds to leave me alone this summer. At first I was worried that I wouldn't know how to breathe. That I'd keep talking to no one in particular, a parrot in sweat pants, asking, "Will I be okay?"

Now I don't care.

I can hear my fingers snapping below me. A small group of old barflies, my unintentional comrades this summer, have gathered around me. They're snapping and dancing too. The sounds of the fingers and the feet echo loudly. More loudly than they usually would because it's very late and the enclosing streets are still. It's

beautiful and it's deafening. After a few seconds I can't hear anything anymore. I can hear my breathing rev up, and that's all.

Some old guy whose name I can't remember is dancing next to
me. He must be copying what I'm doing because when I turn, he
turns, and in a few seconds, we meet again. I must be smiling at
him because he's smiling too. He can feel how happy I am. He
thinks I'm beautiful right now, I know it.

I've never been this happy.

Then the music stops.

The lights flicker and then go on. It's time for me and all the old
drunks in this joint to go home.

I step outside of O'Malley's and light a cigarette.

I'm still sweating from all the dancing inside. I thought stepping
out would feel refreshing, but it doesn't. Fuck, it's hot. Even after
midnight.

I've got to leave quickly tonight, before everyone else. If I linger
too long, the happiness will fade away, drown in conversation. My
happiness is selfish. If I tuck it away for a few moments, it slips past
me, angry that I'm paying attention to someone else. I can't risk
that tonight. I need to be able to paint this feeling tomorrow.

I moved to New York on a scholarship to go to art school. I
flunked out of every class. I had everything I ever wanted and I
was paralyzed. I have become the failure I was always convinced
Michael would make me.

"Bye, Grace!" yells Queen Anne. She's called Queen because she
has a British accent.

The moon acts like a kind spotlight on Queen's face, washing
away all the deep lines. She doesn't look cheap anymore. She looks
elegant, regal even. She glows. She must have been beautiful once.

"Bye, Anne!" I yell back. "I'll see you tomorrow."

I pat my purse one last time, just to make sure I still have everything. I'm forgetting things lately. I never used to do that. I stamp out my cigarette quickly. My feet sting; without the dancing there's no distraction from the pain. Why did I wear high heels tonight? It's a long walk home.

Oh, fuck it. Who needs shoes?

When I turn the corner, the pavement feels smooth and cold beneath my feet. I want to run home, eyes closed.

I used to love running home from school as a very little girl. I used to go so fast that I swore I was flying. I told the other girls at school that I could fly, that I did fly home every day. I was convinced that what moved me, what pushed my feet one in front of the other wasn't me. It was something bigger than me. Something I didn't control. Maybe I did fly.

Running doesn't feel like that anymore. I have to move myself forward. I have to lift my feet. I have to control it. I miss those wings.

My feet sound like horse's hooves beneath me. I turn down my street, opening my eyes.

And then I see him, in the distance. My blood runs cold.

Michael.

My shadowy giant.

He's walking toward me. His broad shoulders, his dark hair, his long legs, all coming closer and closer to me. It's him.

My breath catches in my throat. I take one of my curls and pat it down against my face. I don't want him to see me like this. Not for the first time since everything happened. He isn't going to love me anymore, not like this. My heart beats so quickly. It's like an orchestra in my ears. I can hear his laugh.

He walks closer, and then closer still.

Suddenly he's in front of me. I grab for my purse, my lipstick, anything for him not to see my face.

Only, it's not him.

At least three times a week I think I see him. Every time, I don't. Every time, I'm breathless, consumed by thoughts of what he's like now. It's only been a year since I've seen him, but I'm certain everything's different. Is he working at the bank with his father? What does he wear? What does he watch? Who does he share a bed with?

Can he feel that I still love him?

I cross the street. I don't want to pass this stranger now. Looking at him closer and closer is just making me angry.

I'm crying. When did I start crying?

I kick a small stone on the sidewalk, hard. It ricochets across the dark street, bouncing back and forth, landing in the golden light of a street lamp. It seems brighter than it usually is. The grass beneath it looks glazed.

I realize I'm shaking my head. There's no one to look at me right now, but I've become self-conscious just imagining what someone might say if they saw me, so I straighten up. I try walking more easily. I want to cling to whatever is left of that happiness from earlier.

I'm drunker than I was just a second ago. It's hard to keep my balance, even with my shoes off.

"You just have to put one foot in front of the other and not fall down on the way home, that's all you have do," I tell myself.

That's all I do.

By the time I'm closing the front door behind me, dawn has risen and the sky is a judgmental orange. I close my eyes tightly and lean against the door, still trying to catch my breath.

I'm winded.

Now there's no fucking way I'll be able to paint tomorrow.

It's strange being back home, both good and bad. It reminds of visiting my elementary school when I was halfway through the eighth grade. Everything looked so much smaller than I had remembered. The stairs that were so tiring to walk I could climb in two steps. I was suddenly taller than my old teacher. She looked frail, fragile even. I remember telling my best friend that we weren't possibly as small as the new kids were when we were their age.

It wasn't an altogether unsettling feeling, though. I had new appreciation for the place. I felt proud there. I'd earned being comfortable between those walls. I liked it more than I had remembered.

Being home again, it's not so different. When I'm falling asleep at night, looking around my room, I feel too big for my blankets. Once I'm asleep, though, I don't stir in my bed. I don't have nightmares anymore, not since I've come home. I don't think I dream at all.

Only it doesn't really feel like home. Not how I remembered home feeling, anyway.

I don't miss New York, I don't miss school. I'm smart enough not to look back.

This morning, I am sitting with my mother for breakfast. The heat finally broke and the restaurant feels so cold. I wish I'd brought a sweater.

"Why are you shivering like that?" my mom asks me.

I look up from my plate at her. My whole life, people have told me we look alike. I don't see the resemblance.

"It's cold in here."

We go back to eating, in silence. It's not the silence between two people who don't need to talk anymore. There's a strange universe between us now.

"Do you like your omelette?"

"Yeah, it's fine," she says.

"That's good. The coffee's nice."

She looks at me and smiles, and I smile back, but her stare lingers too long.

"How are your friends?"

"They are all good, getting ready to go back to school."

She nods. I nod. She won't look away.

"Your makeup looks too thick today."

I take my starched cloth napkin, dip it in her water, and move it all over my face.

"Is that better, Mom?"

I watch her now.

"You are such a beautiful girl, Grace. All that makeup just hides how beautiful you are."

I would love another cup of coffee. With the hangovers, headaches are blunt.

"So I think your father and I are going away this weekend. Can you remember to water the plants? Grace?"

"I'm sorry, what, Mom?"

"Are you all right, Grace? You seem out of it." Her eyes narrow and a judgment is passing.

"I'm fine."

There is an edge in my voice; I can feel it more than I can hear it. "Are you hungover?"

"No."

She can still read the nuances of my face, and I can still read the nuances of hers. I know she knows I'm lying.

Before the gloves come off I see Diane, my mother's old friend, and I wave at her. I used to play with Diane's son, Jeremy, but he was a few years younger than me, and I rarely think of him now. He must be almost a man.

"Grace, Susan, how nice to see you both!"

"Nice to see you too, Diane! How is Jeremy?" my mom asks.

"He's great. He's just starting his last year of high school, can you believe it? And he just got his licence. Grace, how are you doing? You must be getting ready to start school again. When are you going back to New York?"

I hate answering that question. I hate it more than anything. When people ask me when I'm going back, I'm reminded that I had to leave in the first place.

"I'm not sure when I'm going back."

"Grace is just taking a bit of a break," my mom offers. She's trying to help me. I should try to appreciate it.

"Oh," says Diane.

There's that look. The look that everyone I know has given me, every single day since I've come back. What happened to her? they are all thinking. What happened to her there that made her come back?

Diane's lips curl into a tight smile, and she looks at me differently than she had before.

"Well, I'll leave you two to your breakfast. It's so nice to see you guys. We should all meet up sometime, have a girls lunch."

"Yeah, we should. Goodbye, Diane," my mom says.

"Bye."

I watch Diane walk away.

"Mom, why did you tell her that? I've told you so many times that I don't want you telling people that."

"What do you want me to do, Grace? Lie?"

"Yes, lie."

"I'm not going to lie."

"Why? I don't want people to know that I'm taking a break. It's embarrassing."

"Grace, whether you want people to know or not, it's very obvious that you are taking a . . . break."

"Why did you say it like that?"

There's the sharpness again. I can feel it and I can hear it.

"Don't speak to me like that. Grace, you are not on a break. You are just getting drunk every night."

"That's not true, Mom."

"What did you do last night?"

"That's not the point."

"What did you do the night before?"

Sadness finds her face and settles around her eyes. I do still know my mother. She's disappointed and confused right now, I can tell. She's staring at me, trying to piece together how I changed from who I was to what I've become. She doesn't like what I've become.

We agree on that.

"I'm doing stuff."

"You are doing nothing."

"She's right," a voice inside me says.

A violent wave of fuchsia feelings crawls up my body. Everything that's inside wants to break through the surface. For the next three seconds I have to push it down. Push it down, don't let it shatter the surface.

"Fuck you."

And with that I'm out of my chair, out of the restaurant, out of my skin. As I'm leaving, I think I hear her ask me where I'm going, but the tears are here and they hurt my eyes and I can't turn back.

The first time I got drunk was with Mike. I was wearing a T-shirt he'd bought me on a rugby trip to the States that said BRUNETTES HAVE MORE FUN. It was something I never would have bought myself, but I was touched that he'd tried. All I'd ever seen him wear was khaki shorts and a sweatshirt, but he noticed that I dressed carefully.

The T-shirt was the farthest thing from me, but it was his attempt at being like me. He considered me avant-garde. I liked his version of myself more than my own.

My head spun. I'd had two drinks and I couldn't stop laughing.

"Are you okay?" he asked. He moved closer to me and put his hand on my thigh.

"Yeah, this is so fun."

He nodded and looked around at the crowd of people around his table drinking, laughing, playing poker.

"I had this party for you."

I held on to him so tight and I don't remember letting go. I know I must have because I ended up being sick on his basement carpet. His dad had to get it replaced and Mike was grounded for a week. I woke up in his bed, wearing the T-shirt. He'd washed my face and covered me in blankets.

"Where did you sleep?" I asked when he shook me gently to wake me just after dawn. He didn't want me to get caught.

"The floor."

He bent over and he kissed me. That day, with my first hangover, I painted a series of portraits all called "Mike" that won me the scholarship.

I gave them to him on his birthday. He sent me an e-mail the day I left for New York telling me he'd left them on my mom's doorstep. If I had been older, even by this one year, I would have hung on.

When I'm outside, I think about all the things that I should've said, that I could've said to my mother.

"You didn't say any of those things because you know everything she said is true," that voice speaks again.

My mother's words repeat and echo in my head, and no matter how hard I try to force them away, they won't leave me. Like stubborn dirt under my fingernails, I can't pick her out. I don't have the wherewithal to fight with her right now. Feelings blur into one, twisting themselves into knots, and bang into each other with force.

Everything around me is moving in slow motion and I'm walking much faster than I should be able to. Time is out of joint. The bricks on the sidewalk mesh together and then with each tear separate again. Eventually I can see nothing but my two feet beneath me.

I need to let these feelings go and put them somewhere else, somewhere concrete. I need to transfer them to something real, something I can touch.

I need to paint.

The shed is musty, still as musty as it was when I left. My breathing is ragged, and I think I should find a seat. Looking around, I see the old yellow lawn chair my dad used to take to my softball games when I was a kid.

"When was the last time someone was in here?" I ask the ceiling.

It's different than I imagined it being, sitting here. I thought it would be more emotional, more frightening. It doesn't really feel like anything.

I don't know how to behave between these walls anymore. I see visions dancing in front of me of how I used to be, but I don't know her anymore. I watch the memories of her move around like I would watch a movie, with a separation and a detachment.

I get up and look at my canvases that Mom has carefully packed up in the corner, hopeful that I'll open them up again.

I used to paint, in silence, for hours at a time. I couldn't tell you where that dedication came from. I'm not sure anyone could. But I felt so close to myself then, going into those strange and secret rooms inside my head and finding new pictures, pulling them out. That part of me is now fully separate from my body. Luckily, it's not a distance that's obvious, a distance that's known. It's subtle. It's numbing.

I see such a brightness in these paintings. I don't feel that brightness inside me anymore.

I used to wonder if my fingertips glowed.

Even in those good times, it felt fleeting. Talent is given, and it can be taken away. I didn't own it. It owned me.

I pick out a blank canvas. It's big, which I'm happy for. I rest it against the wall in front of me and stare at it.

Even before my brush touches the canvas I'm tentative. My arm feels disjointed and not my own. I feel the distance now.

"How did this happen?" I ask myself.

I make a few strokes, but they are cautious. Out of the corner of my eye I can see my old canvases. They mock me now. I will never be able to do anything like them again.

It's because he's gone.

"Stop telling me that," I say to myself

The more I press upon the canvas, the more I hate it. Those paintings in the corner, they were so candid. Now, too many things watch. It's so loud in here.

I stare at my big canvas. I can't see anything between it and my eyes, nothing, just darkness. I'm doubly blind.

I sit down in my old yellow chair. The frustration surrounding me is palpable. It's another person in the shed, only she won't talk to me or keep me company. She just makes her presence known.

"How did this all come undone?" I ask myself.

He took it when I left him.

I don't want to think anymore.

It's five o'clock in the afternoon but that really doesn't matter. Once I'm out of the shed, I feel like I can breathe again. I know the relief is fleeting. If I don't get to the corner as quickly as I can, I will lose my breath, the rug will be pulled from under me, and I'll free-fall, deep and fast.

I am the youngest thing here this evening by decades, but that doesn't matter. I can breathe deeply, and soon with abandon. I sit next to blond Rita, who is always happy to see me, and tell myself that I should wait ten minutes before ordering. I will wait ten minutes before ordering.

Four days out of five, the regulars are the AA crowd, just trying to get sober. I see them some nights outside of local churches, smoking yellowed cigarettes together when their meetings end. I give them a quick wave and they just nod back. I don't want to talk to them so close to God. They know that they don't want to talk to me either. I would just remind them that they are still practising alcoholics.

This summer O'Malley's has become a place of worship for me too. There is no prayer, though, only confession.

My relationship with these people was a kind of ultimate closeness coupled with an infinite distance. And it's that distance that allows us to be so close.

But we don't spend time together sober. There are no shared interests or people. There is no history between us. What would we talk about? I've come to realize that there's little difference between a young drunk and an old drunk. As a young drunk, I'm so honest around them because I'm not constantly afraid I'm going to disappoint them. As old drunks, they are so honest around me because I'm one of the few people they haven't disappointed yet.

They're at those real churches, though, four days out of five. Walking away from them I always marvel at the kind of courage it must take to go to those meetings hungover. I wonder what kind of faith they must have in themselves to really believe that they can quit, one last time and for good. I don't think I could ever face my demons so naked four days out of five.

"How was your day, Gracey?" Rita asks me.

"It was good, Rita. It was good."

I smile at her, and she smiles back. She has a kindness in her eyes.

"What do you want tonight, Grace?" Tom yells at me from behind the bar.

"My usual," I holler back.

"It's been eight minutes," I tell myself.

"Make that a double."

I sit back in my chair. It'll be a few hours before my friends get here but that's fine. I like being here, alone, with these people. There is no one watching.

"How's your summer been?" Dylan asks me.

"It's great." I smile at him. He's sitting close to me. His hand is on my leg, and it's moving up my thigh, which is strange because we don't talk in real life. His hand feels warm. I don't want him to move it.

"Ar-are you still at school?" I ask him.

I know the answer. He isn't still at school. But it's late, and the room is spinning, and I'm not able to remember conversations I've already had. I try to force myself to think about times I've talked to Dylan before but I can't. My thoughts are shallow right now. If I try to wade through them I'll just hit a glass wall that hides the past, and bounce off of it, back into the forefront of my mind. All I'm able to think about is right now, this minute, this second.

The music is loud. I can feel that restlessness in my legs, and I want to move.

"I love this song, Dylan."

I can tell I'm still smiling at him, and I shift my body closer to his, filling what little space was left between us.

"Do you want another drink?" he asks me.

"I can't."

His body feels hard pressed next to mine. Seconds slip past us and I don't know what is supposed to happen next.

"Do you want to get out of here?"

I sneak him in through the back door. I tell him he has to leave before dawn. In my room he looks bigger than he was just moments ago at the bar.

Things are very quiet between us. I don't know why they are so quiet so quickly.

The silence between us is ripe.

Soon there is no pretense, and we aren't polite. He kisses me, and I kiss him back, harder. I want this. I really want this.

He pushes me into a corner, and the surrounding darkness follows. I can't see in front of me, I can just feel him against me. He touches me, without premeditation. Without permission. Without thought.

"You never used to be this beautiful," he tells me.

I don't know what to say back.

"If you really should be doing this, you'd probably know what to say back," the voice tells me.

I pretend I didn't hear it, but I still don't have anything to say.

Time is fragmented and lapses very quickly. I'm bare and he's bare and suddenly there is nothing actual between us.

It hurts at first, but I like the fullness inside me.

When we're finished, he holds me. In the darkness, he doesn't feel different than the one I was used to. His arms are wrapped around my waist just the same, we are sleeping close together just the same, our breathing is in sync. It's almost all just the same. I fall asleep believing it's the one I'm used to next to me. I'm too drunk to remind myself to notice the differences that separate the two.

I wake up hungover, alone, and next to the familiar ghost.

I held off sleeping with Mike for a long time, until we were eighteen.

"I want to get dressed up," I said. "You don't have to."

When he opened his father's door, he was wearing a suit and tie.

"I bought us ice cream sandwiches," he said.

We sat on his couch and watched *24*. When the show ended, he went to the kitchen and he took two shots. He was so nervous he was shaking. He offered me some.

"I'm fine," I said. "I don't need it."

After a while, it hurt too much and so we stopped. He held me and as he fell asleep, I named every shadow on his bedroom wall. They became my companions as he slept soundly and I lay awake dreaming.

The heat came back this morning. It's suffocating. I went walking today with the girls, my friends from high school. They are all home for the summer, and although they indulge like I do, they have somewhere to go back to. Realizing this, slowly but constantly, even laughter felt like a chore. Before I left, the laughter with them was usually so natural. It came in floods, and like fireworks erupting it cascaded loudly above us, swayed and settled around us, eventually falling beneath us, disappearing. Today every inhale, every rise, every fall, every exhale was laboured. It made me tired.

The girls and I have taken to wearing the same skirt, cotton, fitted, black, cinched at the waist. Before I would have hated the thought of dressing like someone else. Now, I don't know how I cared.

Night falls quickly and looking up I don't see any stars. The sky is so dark that I wonder if it could absorb me.

"Do you have a light?" I ask Old Joe.

I used to be scared shitless of Old Joe. He has the gruffness of a man who has lived his life alone, unconcerned with pleasantries. When I was a kid, he used to tell my brother, John, and me that he was an astronaut. We believed him until I was about eight because of the NASA badge sewn to the hat he's worn every day for as long as I can remember. I've spent a lot of time with him this summer. We always seem to find each other outside the bar, looking for a cigarette or an escape. Without a doubt, he's my favourite.

He raises his hand with a gentleness that he saves for when we are alone and lights my cigarette.

"What d-do you want to drink, Miss Grace?"

"I'm taking tonight off, Joe. I'm fine, but thanks."

"I used to take nights off too."

His eyes are a piercing blue, framed by wild white eyebrows. No matter how much he's drunk or how slurred his speech is, there is always a frightening clarity in his gaze. I think that's what scared me when I was young. When he looks into my eyes he can see too much.

"What'd you do today, Joe?"

He clears his throat and rises to put out his smoke. He sways more than usual today. I get up, fast.

"Sit down, girl, I'm fine. I don't need help." I've embarrassed him and I sit back down quicker than I got up. "I came here 'round two this afternoon, so that's what I did today."

"Did I miss anything?"

"Days are changeless at this place, my girl. Nothing happens. What'd you d-do?"

"I saw the girls. We went walking."

"Hot day for walking."

"You're telling me, Joe."

"Ta-take a look at Barbara in there."

Barbara is dancing next to Daniel, who I went to high school with. She moves with a sexuality that is only becoming to a woman much younger than she is.

I laugh hard, and he wheezes and laughs also, pleased. Even though the sun is hiding, the laughter is still exhausting, still laboured.

"So wh-what'd you do today, Gracey?"

"I just told you, Joe."

He looks at me still with clear eyes, but confusion clouds his blue irises.

"N-no you didn't. What'd you do today, Gracey?"

"I went walking with the girls. It was hot."

"A hot day for a walk."

"Yeah, you're telling me, Joe."

I look at my feet. It's not my place to correct him. He gets up again, I'm not sure why. This time he does fall over. I get down next to him and give him my hand.

"Joe, are you okay?"

"Yeah, yeah, girl, I'm fine . . . I-I-I don't know how that happened there. Just lost my feet under me."

He finds his feet again and steadies himself slowly. He is graceful, even in the most graceless situations.

"Did you hurt yourself?"

"Nah, nah. Don't worry about me, Melinda."

"No, Joe, I'm Grace. I'm not Melinda."

He looks at me, and after a few seconds of silent searching, he looks surprised to find out that I am not Melinda.

"Grace! Grace. I-I don't know why I said Melinda. I get mixed up some days. Forgive me."

If he's bringing her up, it's time for him to go home.

"Joe, do you think you want me to walk you home maybe?"

"No! N-n-no! I don't want to go home, Gracey. I'm fine. I got my wits about me, I am just getting on and I f-forget things."

"Okay, okay, I'm sorry. I didn't mean it like that."

"You just remind me a' her, is s'all. She was your age last time I seen her. They're all so pretty when they're your age."

From what I have been able to piece together Melinda was Joe's daughter. I don't know what happened to her, I just know she's not here anymore.

"I bet she was beautiful."

"She was beautiful, just like y-you're beautiful."

"That's really nice of you to say, Joe."

"It's n-not nice, it's true, girl."

The fluorescent light from inside is so bright that it spills out of the bar. It throws a soft light out front, where Joe and I are sitting. In this moment, I can see all the lines around his eyes, all the life he's lived. A peculiar stillness finds us, and it transforms his face. He looks away from me and there's a long moment before he finds words.

"Th-they say people don't recover from things like that. Th-that's not all true. You recover in some ways, you keep on recoverin'. You just don't ever get fixed. I'm n-not ever gonna get fixed."

He takes a swig of his beer.

My voice and my face behave, or will themselves to behave, like this is a normal conversation.

"I'm sorry."

The sight of Joe's face, the grief and the sadness in it, hurts to look at. I put my hand on his shoulder, and I look away.

I think I should go home.

I call Michael without thinking. My fingers sail around the numbers instinctively and hold the phone to my ear without shaking. I watch myself and our conversation from outside of my body. It's someone else speaking to him, and I'm just listening in.

"I need to see you."

"Okay," he says.

I hang up after a few moments. The familiarity coupled with how long it's been since I spoke to him last act like a sinking rock in my stomach. I'm anchored.

I don't regret being so thoughtless.

My mouth feels dry. Even though we've been looking at menus for over five minutes, there is nothing that I want to eat when the waitress comes to take our order.

"What are you having?" I ask him. My voice sounds like it's floating, lingering high above us.

"Western with cheese."

"Yeah, okay, I'll have the same."

He looks different than he used to. He's aged, and not how I thought he would. I only recognize him when he smiles, and even then it's only because I'm searching for what I used to see. I've spent so much time remembering. The little details that I was careful not to let fade away, that I held on to so tightly, don't exist in the flesh. Not how they're supposed to.

"I heard you came back earlier, in the spring."

"Yeah, I just wanted to come home. How's work?"

"It's okay. I mean, I hate it, but the money is decent. Why is your hair straight?"

"Oh, I just thought you'd like it."

I want to touch him how I used to. I can still feel his hands all over me, his breath on my face, his lips on mine. I can feel him inside me, but I can't reach out and touch him. I'm not allowed. There's a formality and stiffness between us. I don't like it.

I look at him and smile. I've rehearsed this so many times, but every word I practised just spins around my head and can't find its way out of my mouth. Thoughts and words get caught in my throat, stuck between my tongue and my teeth.

"When did you get glasses, Mike? I didn't know that you had glasses."

"Yeah, the doctor told me I needed them."

"I like them."

"Thanks."

I can tell he's waiting for me to start. He keeps looking away from me and fixing his hat. He's nervous. He doesn't know why I've asked him here.

He's finished eating and I haven't touched my food.

"Just say it, Grace," I tell myself.

He looks up at me, and I can tell he's trying hard not to see me. He doesn't want to see me. Not the way he used to see me, as the girl that he loved. I don't want to tell him everything anymore. Not if he's not really looking at me.

"Why did you need to talk to me, Grace?" There's anger in him. It's subtle but it burns under the surface.

"You just have to tell him, that's all you have to do," I tell myself.

There's a pause, and he's still looking at me, but his face is so genuine now. Looking at him I see his primordial cells, everything I've lost.

"I miss you. Every second. I think about you all the time, and

I don't want to, and I ignore it but I can't stop myself. It just gets worse and worse, Michael. Everywhere I look I see you. I see us, and for the tiniest moments it's not true, and everything didn't get all fucked up, and we still are the way we were, the way we're supposed to be. And it wasn't this bad at first. I was okay, at first. But it gets worse, and I feel . . . everything feels so wrong without you. I don't know what to do without you. I'm so fucked without you. I'm so angry at myself because I should be in New York and I should be painting . . . but I couldn't be there and I can't do anything that I used to without you. There is such a space everywhere and it follows me, and it's what you used to fill."

I've said it. The words leapt out of my mouth, across the table, and they sink on him. He doesn't say anything back.

"I don't know what you want me to say here, Grace."

"I don't want you to say anything."

I ruined it all. I didn't say that right. I should have said that differently.

"You broke up with me, Grace."

"I know. I know I did. I felt like I had to . . . I don't think I wanted to. I made mistakes. I know I make it hard. I know that I did things wrong."

"I wanted to work it out. I tried so many times to make it better. You didn't want to make it better. You didn't want . . ."

There's a vulnerability now, though, and he's letting himself look at me, and really see me for the first time this afternoon. In this moment, I know that everything that was once between us still exists. It feels real between us, we're connected again. Like we're just Grace and Mike again.

"I still love you, Mike."

"Why are you doing this now? When I knew things were ending, when I knew things were going to end, even before everything happened . . . it's been so long now. I had to work so hard."

"I know it was hard. It was for me too. But it's not getting easier, and maybe if it's not getting easier then it wasn't supposed to have happened in the first place."

"I don't know."

"What don't you know?"

We sit across from each other just a few feet apart, but I feel like there's an ocean between us. I'm looking at him and he's looking at me, but neither one of us speaks.

He looks down and away from me for a very long time. He's struggling.

"There's someone else, Grace."

"What?" I ask, and everything blurs around me. I want to double over. I can't see anything. I just burn. Burn, under the white hot heat.

Does he love her?

"Do you love her?"

"I don't know. I think so . . . I want to. Grace, don't cry."

"I'm not crying."

"Please don't cry, Grace."

"But what about us? We were so happy, Mike."

"That's the way we were."

"What does that mean? What about now?"

He won't say anything.

"So, for you, this is just . . . done?"

"I can't do it all again."

All I can see is white light. Blunt, burning, blistering, white light.

"I'm sorry."

But it's too late.

That light is searing.

My dad is in the front room.

One afternoon, not long ago, I saw a man I thought might be him, sitting on a patio. I couldn't be certain because I could only see his back. He was balder than I thought. He looked smaller and older. This man in a red sweater, sitting all alone, he seemed so kind. Only as I walked closer did I realize that it was my dad. The differences between the new man I saw and my dad disappeared, and I could just see my father.

For the briefest of moments, I had seen him with new eyes, as someone who didn't know him would see him. To look at someone you are so familiar with as a stranger is a moving experience. Especially when the first things you notice are good things. Since that day, I have felt closer to my father than ever before.

He's been a silent observer this summer. I don't see him very often, but he never makes me feel stupid for being different. Maybe I'm not different to him.

Today I can tell he knows there is something very wrong, but he doesn't ask me anything.

I collapse in his arms, and I cry in a way that I haven't before, and probably will never again.

"Don't tell anyone," I say.

He won't.

My brush touches the canvas. Grey glides up and down the white surface.

At first the darkness looks mysterious and beautiful, in silhouette. Filling it in, layering the darkness, is more complicated.

It is sharp and unforgiving, but I can still see a gentle kindness in the shadows.

Mama

Cheryl lies naked and cold in her bed.

She has just turned twenty-six and is still drunk from her birthday party. She didn't think she would be sleeping alone tonight.

Her phone rings. She picks up at 4:45 AM, even though she shouldn't, because how would she know who was calling? "Caller ID takes the fun out of phone calls," that's what she always said. But really, she likes thinking it's him calling, and not being reminded that he rarely does.

Hoping it's him now, the man who left her alone tonight, she answered the phone.

"Hi."

"Cheryl-Lee?"

"Yes?"

A woman. She doesn't recognize the voice.

"It's Aunt Lori."

Cheryl-Lee sits up. Why is Aunt Lori calling so late? Why is Aunt Lori calling at all?

"Aunt Lori. Hi."

Cheryl-Lee slurs her words. She focuses on sounding sober.

"Sweetheart, I'm sorry for calling so late. I'm sorry it's so late."

"What's . . . what is it?"

"Your mama's dead."

Nothing moves in Cheryl-Lee's body.

"What?"

"Your mama . . . she's dead."

Cheryl-Lee says nothing.

"Heaven took her, took her we think yesterday."

Cheryl-Lee still says nothing.

"Earl found her in the apartment just past midnight. We kept calling her and she wasn't picking up, so I made Earl go. He found her . . . and I'm sorry, Cheryl-Lee."

Aunt Lori starts crying.

Cheryl-Lee doesn't.

"Was she drinking?" Cheryl-Lee asks.

Aunt Lori says nothing for a moment.

"I don't know."

"Okay."

Cheryl-Lee turns her head and looks around her apartment. It's dark and she can only see shadows. I have no idea what to do, she thinks. What am I supposed to do?

"Sweetheart, I am so sorry," Aunt Lori says between soft cries.

Ask about the funeral.

"When is the funeral?"

"Monday, we think Monday."

"Okay. I'll take a train out Sunday morning."

"I was hoping, I was hoping . . ."

"What?"

"You can stay with me, okay? Me and Earl, we have that extra bedroom, so you can stay here. But you need to stay for a few days, I'd think. Your mama had a lot of stuff we'll need to look through. So I was hoping you'd come earlier. Probably stay for a week, but don't worry about getting a hotel. You'll stay here."

Fuck, a week?

"Uh, I don't know, I'd need to get off work and . . ."

"I'd think they'd understand, Cheryl-Lee. They would at a time like this."

Cheryl-Lee is too drunk to think of another way to get out of going home for a week.

"Okay. When do you want me to come?"

"Tomorrow."

Fuck, thinks Cheryl again, only this time the word vibrates through her whole body. Tomorrow. I have to go home tomorrow.

"I'll call you when I'm on the way to the station."

"I'm so sorry, sweetheart."

Aunt Lori cries a little harder. Cheryl still doesn't know what to do.

"Okay," she says.

Aunt Lori says goodbye and that she loves her and apologizes once more for calling so late.

She lies down. She's naked and cold and drunk.

"Mama's dead," she says out loud.

They haven't spoken in ten years.

At dawn, Cheryl-Lee is still naked, cold, alone.

She had called him right after she found out, two hours ago. "I'll be there right away," he said.

When the birds started, she got up, made coffee, got dressed, and started packing. She threw whatever wasn't dirty into a small suitcase she had bought for a vacation to the West Coast that she and Ben would take. They never did.

After she filled it with the few conservative clothes she owned, but never wore, she undressed and went back to bed.

There was no way she could face leaving until he showed up. No way in hell.

And that was the difficult part. He would show up. She knew he would; he always did.

He was there, but just barely, and so Cheryl was never forced to let him go. And yet, she couldn't let him in either because he wasn't really hers. He was a greying apparition, made only of wispy smoke.

But she held him with her teeth, clinging to him as he drifted away, clinging to the hope that he might change, chewing on what was never there to begin with. Every time she was about to let go, he could tell. He dragged her back, kicking and screaming.

It was violent, their love.

Finally, when the sun peeked through the sheers on her window and light fell onto her bed, making her warm, he showed up.

"I'm sorry."

"Where were you?"

He looks at her. His clothes are wrinkled. He looks guilty.

He was with his wife.

"I'm sorry," he says again.

"There is no reason to be sorry." Some things are too far gone to be sorry about.

She rolls over on her worn sheets and turns her back to him. He moves past her suitcase and the mess, lying with her on her bed. He smells like a perfume she'd never wear. Cheryl feels tired on the inside.

"Are you okay?" he whispers.

"Yeah . . . I don't know."

"I'm sorry."

"Yeah."

"What happened?"

"I don't know yet. She was probably drunk."

He holds her.

"I don't want to go home," she says after a while.

"I know."

"I just can't . . . I don't know if I can do it."

"I know."

"Will you come with me?" she asks.

He doesn't say anything. He just breathes next to her.

"I'm serious, Ben. Please come with me."

He shakes his head.

"Why not?"

"Because you know I can't. I can't do that."

"Right."

She says nothing. He says nothing. They lie together.

"Can you do me a favour?" she asks.

She feels him nod against her, his stubble on her bare shoulder.

"Tell me that you don't love me."

"What?"

"Just say it, Ben. Just tell me."

"You know I can't say that."

It's been two years. Two fucking years, thinks Cheryl, and he won't even be my date for my mother's funeral.

"Don't laugh, Cheryl."

"Why?" He is under her skin, crawling around. "Please come with me," she whispers.

He looks at her. He's more wrinkled than he was when they first met. He's older, fatter, in some places different but unchanged. This will never change, she thinks.

He will always let her down, and she will always set herself up for the fall.

"I can't," he says.

"Then kiss me like you missed me."

Cheryl knows that these are the moments, after your mother has died and your relationship is ending, when you should cry. But she doesn't feel like crying. She doesn't feel anything at all.

He doesn't kiss her.

"I have to go to the bar and tell them I'm taking a week off."

She turns her back to him again and gets dressed. After a minute or two, she leaves. As she hears her high heels and her steady measured gait against the wood floor, a walk born from a lot of leaving behind, she prays that this is it. That it can be over, that she can let it be over, this time for good.

He was never even here to begin with, she thinks.

"Be gone by the time I'm back," she says.

She closes the door behind her.

How the fuck is she going to tell him she's pregnant now?

"Listen, man, I know I'm boning you here, but I need to get a week off."

Cheryl is standing at her boss's door. His name is Greg. She's just woken him up, and he's pissed off and confused. Nine o'clock is ungodly for anyone who works in bars. He's just gotten a haircut, his first one in five years, because he's getting married to his girl in two weeks.

Greg has known Cheryl since she was twenty-one, when she first started at the bar. He's good to her. He helps her when she needs it. They're friends, real friends. She has few.

"I can't just give you a week off, Cheryl."

"Look, I wouldn't ask unless I really needed it."

"Well, why do you really need it? What happened? Did someone die or something?" He laughs, attempting to make a joke but deciding it's too fucking early to follow through.

Cheryl says nothing. She lights a cigarette.

"What happened?" He knows it's serious.

"I don't want to talk about it, okay? Just give me the week."

"Cheryl, tell me what happened," he says, now very serious.

She sighs, angry. She has to tell him if she wants the week off. She looks up and exhales a large, silver cloud of smoke.

"My mom."

He looks at her with a sickening pity. She's never seen him look so sorry for anything, and it scares her.

"Fuck. Cheryl, I'm so . . ."

"No. No, Greg. None of that. Don't feel sorry for me. I hated her, you know that. We didn't talk, it's fine. I'm not sad."

"I know but . . ."

"Look, stop. She's dead and I have to go home, to deal with it. So that's what I'm doing."

He won't stop looking at her.

"This is why I didn't want to tell you," she says.

"Okay. Is anyone going with you?"

"You mean Ben? Yeah. Right."

She laughs, always when she shouldn't. Greg doesn't. He puts his hand on her shoulder.

"You can be upset about this, Cheryl."

"Oh, Greg, fuck off. I'm serious. I'm just taking a week off, okay?"

"Okay."

"Thanks."

As she's walking away he calls after her.

"Do you want me to come with you for a couple days?"

"No. Thank you, but no."

"With your dad, I felt bad when you went back home alone. I should have gone with you then."

"That was different, I was twenty-two. And I liked him."

"Okay."

She walks farther down the block.

"One more thing, Cheryl! One more thing."

"What, Greg?" she yells, turning back.

"Cover up your tattoos when you go home. And your tits! They're busting out over there."

This is genuinely his idea of being helpful, thinks Cheryl.

"Get fucked, Greg."

She gives him the finger as she walks down his street.

"I'm pregnant!" she yells back to him, at the last moment, just before she's out of sight.

He laughs. He thinks she's joking.

When she goes home to pick up her bags, Ben's gone. No note. No nothing. She changes into a blouse that covers her chest piece. Since she feels like walking, she drags her suitcase behind her all the way to the station, the scraping sound loud behind her on the quiet morning streets.

On the way, Cheryl wishes she could call her father.

"Mom died," she'd say.

"I heard," he'd say.

"You get the same hysterical call from Lori?" she'd ask.

"Yeah," he'd say, raspy, slow, steady.

They'd be dates for the funeral, going for a farmer's breakfast after and ordering beer with it. They'd end up laughing at how morbid they look, dressed in black.

She wonders what he would think, if he could see her now: pregnant, aimless, in love with a ghost. What would he think, if he'd seen everything that happened since he'd gone?

Then she wonders if Daddy's waiting for Mama in heaven. They separated years ago, but maybe he's still waiting for her. She hopes he's waiting for her.

"Grow up," she tells herself, disgusted for thinking like that, for being so sentimental.

It doesn't work that way.

"So what brings you to Wellington?" asks the blue-haired old lady Cheryl-Lee sits across from on the train. She thinks the lady's name is Ethel or Marge, but she can't remember because she wasn't really listening.

"My mother died," says Cheryl-Lee. Then she smiles.

The old lady's hand comes to her mouth.

"I am so sorry."

"Thanks."

The lady reaches her hand over and puts it on Cheryl's knee.

"We were estranged."

Cheryl moves her knee.

"Oh," says the lady and nods like she understands. "Oh . . . well, that's, I'm sorry."

The lady looks like she wants to ask what happened but knows it would be impolite. Instead, she sits silently, looking like she pities Cheryl.

"She was a drunk. And I hated her for it."

The lady looks shocked.

Cheryl sighs and rests her head against the train window. She's tired. She's hungover. She wishes Ben were here.

She hears the lady porter ask her if she'd like coffee or snacks. She doesn't turn to say no. She feels wholly glued to the glass separating her from the outside, where everything blends together in a blur of green, sky, tracks.

Soon, she starts to recognize the scenery and her anxiety kicks in. She reaches in her bag, scraping lipsticks, money, smokes, and miscellaneous shit she should have thrown away years ago.

Where the fuck are her pills?

How could she forget her pills?

She thinks of ways she can get out of going home. She could get off at the next stop. She could jump off the train. She can't do this without her pills.

As the train inches closer and closer to home, sick is rising. She's sweating. Maybe it's the baby that's making her sick.

Cheryl's only two weeks late. She figures she has a good month before she needs to make any decisions.

Her eyes feel heavy. She needs to go to sleep. Maybe there's some doctor in town I can scam for pills, she thinks. She turns, avoiding eye contact with the old lady, and rests her head against the other side of her seat. She wakes up when the train rolls into the station.

On her way to the platform, she is hit by a sudden wave of nausea. She vomits, twice, in the train's washroom.

No place like home, she thinks as she raises her face out of the toilet bowl, shaking as she wipes the puke from the corner of her mouth.

With a sour mouth, she calls Lori and writes down her address again because the piece of paper is lost in her purse. That could have been an excuse to turn around, she thinks.

She hangs up and, with ink staining her hand, tries to hail a taxi outside the train station.

Her insides feel empty when the smell hits her. It smelled the exact same way when she left. Like fresh-cut grass and tar. Burning tar. How can a place smell the same ten years later? It's not fair that it smells the exact same. She feels sixteen again and all she wants to do is run.

The air is thick. It's going to be a hot week, she can tell. She's nauseous again.

She gets in the taxi and tries to undo the window. It's jammed.

"Excuse me?"

"Yeah?"

The taxi driver is a middle-aged white man with no accent. Only here, she thinks.

"Does this window work? It's really hot back here."

"Oh yeah, that hasn't worked for a good while now. Sorry."

"Can you open your window up there?"

He laughs.

"Ha! I can try. Don't think it'll do you any good."

He opens his window and she feels hotter.

"So what brings you to Wellington?"

"I don't want to talk," she says, trying with everything she has not to puke.

He looks at her in the rear-view mirror and rolls his eyes.

All she wants is to be anywhere but here.

Cheryl-Lee is bear-hugged by Lori, or someone she thinks might be Lori. She'd ask, but she can't breathe.

The possible Lori met her as she was getting out of the cab. She ran from her porch toward her like a bat out of hell. Cheryl, frightened by this stranger flying toward her, moved back against the cab.

"Oh my God! You haven't changed one bit!" says the woman as she hugs her.

Hearing her loud, hoarse voice, she knows for certain it's Lori. Jesus, she got fat.

"Lori, I was sixteen the last time you saw me. I think I've changed," she says, gasping for air.

"No! Honest, not one bit!"

"Well . . . thanks."

Cheryl finally struggles free. Lori takes her by the shoulders and looks at her.

"Cheryl-Lee, you are certainly a sight for sore eyes. I'm just . . . I'm just so sorry about . . . your mama and—"

Before she can finish her sentence, Lori bursts into tears. Cheryl doesn't know what to do with this sobbing, fat woman she spent childhood Christmases and Thanksgivings with.

"I just, oh, I am so sorry, I just, you know . . . your mama, this whole thing has hit me hard . . . but Jesus has her now, I just tell myself that Jesus has her now. But I just, I just wish . . . I wish . . ."

Lori cries so hard she chokes. Cheryl looks around, hoping to see anyone who can stop the crying. Then she puts her hand on Lori's round shoulder.

"It's okay." Her voice is so monotone she doesn't even believe herself.

Lori wipes her tears, misses the snot under her nose.

"I know. I know it will be okay. It's just so good to have you back, Cheryl-Lee. I'm just sorry things stayed how they were with you and your mama."

"It's Cheryl, now. Call me Cheryl."

Lori looks taken aback.

"Oh, okay. Cheryl."

Cheryl pays the cabbie and gets her bag out of the trunk.

"Do you need help with that there?" asks Lori.

"No."

"Cheryl, look, I'm sorry I'm such a mess . . ."

Shit, she's crying again.

"It's okay," says Cheryl. "Death's hard."

Maybe there is a Motel 6 or something down the road, thinks Cheryl. She looks down the driveway at her aunt's house. The sight of it takes her breath away. It looks the exact same. The brick is still unfinished, the grass is still brown, the same junk litters the driveway.

Cheryl wants to keel over. It's not fair that everything looks exactly the same.

"Is Earl home?" Cheryl asks, still staring at the house.

"No. He's out getting some food for lunch. I wanted to stay and see you."

There's no way she can face a meal with these people yet.

"What bedroom am I in?"

"The one you always had when you stayed over."

Great.

"Oh, okay. I'll just take this up there and get settled then. I'm going to try to take a nap."

"Okay, sweetheart. I think I'll just sit out here and wait for Earl, with this nice weather and all."

Lori wipes her eyes again.

As Cheryl turns around and walks up the driveway, Aunt Lori yells, "Do you want me to wake you for dinner?"

No.

"Sure."

"Okay, see you at supper then!"

She's almost in the door when she hears, "Cheryl-Lee! Oh! Sorry! Cheryl!"

"Yeah?"

"It is so good to have you back."

Save me, thinks Cheryl. Please save me.

Cheryl is in Lori's bathroom on the second floor. She is sitting on the edge of the bathtub trying to calm her breathing. The porcelain feels cold against her thighs. She wishes she had her pills.

She gets up, lights a smoke, opens the window just a crack, and moves back to the tub.

She looks at herself in the mirror. She notices the wallpaper is the same. White, with blue flowers, only wrinkled and browned with age. She used to hide in here, between the bathtub and the corner, from her mother.

Mama went raging mad when she got too drunk. Cheryl learned fast when it was best to hide from her mama. So when Mama and Lori really got going, she would hide between the bathtub and the wall.

Once she got into the position she couldn't move her legs much. Skinny, with knock-knees and long blond hair, Cheryl-Lee would pretend she was a princess hiding from a dragon, waiting for her prince to save her. She made sure to be very quiet and only get up if she really had to use the toilet. Mama never found her.

One night, Mama came into the bathroom. Cheryl-Lee didn't understand why she walked all the way up the stairs when there was a bathroom below, but that night, she did. Mama didn't notice her. Too drunk, Cheryl-Lee guessed.

What's more, Mama didn't use the toilet. Instead, she just stared at herself in the mirror, the same mirror Cheryl is looking in now, and started crying. It was quiet crying, but Mama stayed there for a long time. Cheryl had never seen her cry before. Mama was not a woman who cried. Neither is Cheryl.

She must have been five or six at the time. It's her most vivid memory of her mother. She never stopped looking at her reflection, didn't even blink, just kept staring and kept crying.

A part of her wanted to help her mother, to hug her, to make her stop crying, but the other part of her knew she couldn't give up her hiding spot, not if she wanted to be safe in the future. So she watched, for what felt like forever. Finally Lori yelled up to Mama, asking if she wanted another drink.

Mama snapped out of it. She moved from the mirror, patted her hair down, and threw water on her face. Then she yelled back that, yes, she wanted vodka.

Now that's what Cheryl drinks, but it still makes her sick when she has to serve it at the bar. When she drinks it, it moves like poison through her, but she craves it more than she's craved anything in her life. Familiarity, she guesses.

Cheryl pulls herself off the tub and ashes her smoke in the toilet, still looking in the mirror. She's not exactly beautiful. She wears too much makeup, and her face possesses a strange masculinity that is not off-putting but not inviting either. Her skin leathery from tanning beds is like a protective armour encasing her bones. She is a natural blonde but for years has dyed her hair jet black like the midnight sky, and it's growing out now.

She turns on the tap. She's thirsty but she can't find a glass. She bends down and drinks from the tap, like she used to.

Then she leaves the bathroom and heads to the bedroom she used when Lori was successful in convincing Mama that she was too drunk to drive home. The house still smells like mothballs, thinks Cheryl.

In the hallway, she sees a black-and-white picture of her mama hanging, crooked, next to a framed bible verse. It's Mama sitting on the lap of some man Cheryl doesn't recognize. She wears fire-engine red lipstick and laughs for the camera. Aunt Lori sits next to her. They must be about the age Cheryl is now.

Mama looks happy. In her leather jacket and with her wild hair, she is almost beautiful. Cheryl shifts her gaze and reads the bible verse.

It reads: "No one is righteous; Romans 3:9–20."

When Cheryl lies in bed she can't sleep until she pretends Ben is holding her.

She never has to do that when she has her pills.

"You know, you look just like your mama did when she was your age."

"Not really."

"Yes, identical. It's like Shannon is just right here, ain't it, Earl?"

"That's true. You do look like her," says Earl.

"She was fatter than I am."

"No, not when she was your age. You're the spittin' image of her. I swear, it took my breath away when you got out of that cab."

"Cool."

"Do you want more there, sweetheart? You're not eating much tonight."

Looking down at a plate that's still crowded with macaroni and stuffing, Cheryl wonders when it would be a good time to mention she's allergic to wheat.

"No, I'm full."

"Oh, okay."

Aunt Lori smiles warmly.

Earl gets up and excuses himself from the table. Cheryl only knew Earl for a few months before she left. He's Lori's third or fourth husband, Cheryl can't remember. Cheryl doesn't mind Earl. He's quiet and he wasn't around for most of the shit that went down. She's got nothing to hold against him. After he's left the room, Lori looks at Cheryl, very serious.

Here we go.

"I know you don't want to be here, but it really means a lot to me, and I know it would to your mama too."

Cheryl nods.

"You know, she made a lot of mistakes, but she was really trying to get better before, well, before she passed."

"Was she still drinking?"

Lori is quiet for a moment.

"Sometimes. Less than she did. She was going to church a lot more too. She had an illness, Cheryl."

"We all have illnesses, Lori."

"She was trying hard to get right with God. She accepted Jesus Christ as her personal saviour. She let him into her heart. She was trying to get better, believe me."

Cheryl laughs.

"That's rich." Cheryl gets up to get some water from the kitchen.

"I know you wrote her off, but I never did. She wasn't as bad as you remember her to be."

Cheryl wants to get a gun and shoot herself. Glass in hand, she turns back to Lori.

"Look, I'm here right now because it's the right thing to do and because you asked me to come. I'm not here because I want to make Mama out to be some saint. So this can all just stop."

"I know, but she was your mama, and she really loved you—"

"I buried her a long time ago," says Cheryl.

Lori stares at Cheryl, looks hurt and wounded, and like it's the saddest thing in the world that everything has turned out the way it has. Cheryl feels a lot of things in this moment—guilty, sad, angry, alone—but she doesn't want to identify them; the velocity at which they are all travelling is frightening.

"Okay?" Cheryl says finally.

"Okay," whispers Lori.

Lori gets up from the table and clears her dishes. She goes to the fridge, pulling something out. Cheryl stares at the wall, numb.

I want a fucking drink.

"Do you want some pie, honey?"

Cheryl wonders if it was Shakespeare who said cowards die a thousand times before their death.

It's eleven-thirty and Cheryl can't sleep, which is no surprise. As soon as she lay down, her skin felt itchy and on fire. She tried telling herself that there was no reason to feel itchy, but no matter how she moved it wouldn't stop. It made her want to rip her skin off her bones. Eventually, she decided to get up and pace the kitchen. Pacing makes her feel calm. She brings her cellphone downstairs with her.

She knows Ben's up. He's just finished work at the restaurant. He'll be walking home. She gets to the kitchen, paces in the darkness. Then she dials his number.

Ring. Ring. Ring.

Why isn't he picking up?

Ring. Ring. Ring.

He knows where she is. Why the fuck isn't he picking up?

He's not going to pick up. He's going to let it go to message.

How can he let it go to message knowing where she is?

"Cheryl? Is that you?" It's Earl.

"Oh, hi, Earl. Sorry. I just couldn't sleep."

Earl walks into the kitchen and turns on the light. He's fully dressed. He goes into the fridge and gets himself a glass of milk.

"That's fine, I'm not one for sleeping either."

He drinks his milk, staring at Cheryl. He won't look away.

"So? Who you calling?" he asks.

"Just no one. It's no one, really."

He nods. He knows she's a liar.

"Well, it's my, ah, he's my boyfriend, but it's a little complicated right now."

"I see."

Cheryl starts pacing again.

"You like pacing, huh?"

"Yeah, it's stupid. It calms me, though." Especially when I don't have my fucking pills, she thinks.

"I get it. Your mama was the same."

Cheryl stops.

"Oh shit, yeah. She paced a track in my kitchen almost. Calmed her down something big."

Cheryl still feels like she needs to pace, but she doesn't want to, not anymore. She tries to remember Mama pacing when she was a kid. She can't.

Earl looks her up and down.

"You look like you want to go out."

"Earl!" the whole bar yells when they walk through the front door.

They're at Cap'n Jacks, smack in the middle of town. They listened to Willie Nelson on the drive over, so Cheryl is happy that the Kinks are playing as she walks in. The bar is lively, crowded with locals.

Cheryl remembers it's Saturday, and she figures this must be the regular crowd. The urge to pace goes away when she sits down in a dirty, damp leather booth.

She looks around for a face she might recognize, then realizes she wouldn't recognize anyone anymore. She used to come here almost every weekend, once she was old enough to wear a push-up bra and smoke.

She thinks she lost her virginity in one of the bathroom stalls here but can't remember. She remembers bleeding after. So, yeah, must have been the first.

She doesn't remember who it was. Not the face, not the name. It was rough, so he must have been older.

"Did you like that?" he asked when they finished.

She knows she nodded, but she couldn't speak afterwards. Too fucked on E.

But it looks a little different in here than she remembers, thank God. It's the one place in all of Wellington that's changed in ten years. Well, it's been painted, anyway. It smells like fake strawberries masking cigarette smoke. It used to smell like piss.

She turns and watches Earl order their drinks at the bar. The bartender looks over Earl's shoulder and motions to her and then turns back to Earl.

"Shannon's daughter?" he mouths.

Earl nods.

She turns around and waits for her vodka. She's not thinking about what's in her stomach until this week is done. A few drinks aren't going to hurt it. Didn't hurt her. Cheryl figures Mama was shitfaced during her whole pregnancy.

"Here you go, miss."

"Thanks, Earl. What do I owe you?"

"Yeah, right."

Cheryl smiles.

"Thank you."

The vodka burns going down, but as soon as it hits her lips she feels her shoulders sink. She focuses on not thinking about the baby.

"So, tell me about yourself," Earl says.

"What?"

"You been real quiet about yourself. I haven't seen you for ten years. Don't you think I'm curious about what you've been up to?"

"No, I didn't think you would be," Cheryl says honestly.

"Come on, now. Start by telling me where you're living."

"Toronto."

"Yeah, I know. What part?"

"Near College. The rent's cheap, and it's close to work so I like it."

"And where's work?"

"I work at a bar. It's called Nirvana. It's nice, gets a lot of traffic. I've been there forever, so it's easy. It's a job."

He waits, drinks his beer.

"You go to school?"

"No. I mean, yeah, I did go to school. I went to some night classes and stuff, but I never finished a degree."

"Why not?"

"I never found anything that I wanted to do, actually."

Earl is quiet and looks at Cheryl like he's taking her in. It makes her uncomfortable.

"I mean, not like in a forever sense. I still don't really know. Or I'm still trying to figure it out."

"And you're just at the bar for now?"

"I guess. You could say that, yeah."

Cheryl wonders when "just for now" turns into forever.

"So tell me about this boyfriend."

"Can we talk about something else?" asks Cheryl, taking off her jacket. She figures she can show some skin in here.

"Really?"

"No. Ah, he's, well, I don't know if he's my boyfriend anymore."

"Right. How long you been together?"

"Two years, I guess. Two years and change, off and on."

"You didn't want to bring him here, I guess?"

"He wouldn't come with me."

Earl looks at Cheryl. He doesn't say anything.

"It's complicated," she says.

"Where'd you meet him?"

"At the bar. He used to work there. It was supposed to be just, not for long, but here we are, two years in. I don't know . . . how it happened, really."

He'd stolen the heart, beating, from her chest.

"Well, I hope it works out."

Cheryl waits, then speaks.

"I don't. I hope it ends. For real this time."

"Then I hope it ends for real this time."

Earl smiles.

Cheryl smiles, but only a little and not for long. The vodka has loosened her, just a bit, and she has to ask him something.

"Earl, can you just, just level with me for a second?"

"Yeah?"

"How'd it happen with Mama? And just tell me. Don't give me any Jesus bullshit like Lori. Just tell me."

Earl takes a sip of his beer. He looks like what he is about to tell her pains him. Cheryl feels suddenly nervous, wishing she hadn't asked.

"She was drunk. She lived alone, and no one was there to help her. She fell down the stairs."

"Are you bullshitting me?"

"What do you mean?" He looks at the table.

He doesn't say anything.

"Earl, look at me."

He looks at her.

"Your mama didn't do it, if that's what you're asking. She fell," is all he says.

Hearing how it really happened hurts her in a new and unexpected way. She doesn't let it show.

"I'm sorry," he says.

"Can you smoke in here?"

Earl nods.

Cheryl lights her smoke.

"You know, this isn't what you want to hear, but she talked about you every day."

"Okay," says Cheryl, exhaling.

"I mean it. Every day she talked about you, how good you were when you were a little girl. The games you used to play alone in your room. She would sing that song you really liked, I'd catch her singing it to herself, that Bob Dylan song."

"'Don't Think Twice,'" says Cheryl without blinking.

"Yeah. 'Don't Think Twice.' Anyway, I know you two didn't talk much, but I wanted you to know that she still thought of you. All the time."

"Okay."

"Shannon meant well. She did."

Cheryl laughs. Always when she shouldn't.

"What?" asks Earl.

"I don't know why you're all so hell bent on me forgiving her. She's dead now."

Cheryl puts out her smoke. She wants another drink.

"I think she wanted to make things right with you."

Cheryl likes Earl. He is the one person she likes in this whole town, and so she wants to tell him how wrong he is.

"I was sixteen when I left. She didn't even try to fix it. So that's bullshit. I don't need . . . you don't need to tell me this to feel better. I got fine with it a long time ago."

"She did try."

"Not hard enough. Not after everything she did. She didn't try hard enough," Cheryl says, venom in her throat.

Earl looks down.

"I'm sorry. It's not my place. I shouldn't be saying any of this."

"It just really gets me that she started going to church. What'd she think? Jesus would make all of her bullshit okay?"

"You don't believe in God?"

"No. Absolutely not. I absolutely do not believe in God."

Earl starts laughing.

"What? Why's that funny?"

"Your mama didn't either. She said all that about accepting Jesus Christ in her heart to make Lori happy. I could tell. She didn't believe. Not for one second."

Cheryl stumbles up the stairs, trying her best to be quiet and not wake Lori. Earl decided to stay outside and smoke one last cigarette before coming in. Dizzy and drunk, she needs to go to bed as quickly as possible. If she waits and sobers up, even a little, she won't be able to sleep tonight.

Cheryl passes Mama's picture on the way to her bedroom. Then she moves back and stares at it for a long, still moment.

We do look alike, thinks Cheryl. So much alike. We smile the same way. Our eyes are the same shape. Her face is round like mine. We sit the same, straight-backed and never comfortable. A pain I inherited and now wear as my own.

Cheryl watches her vision blur, then focus. She's crying. She can't remember the last time she cried.

She puts her hand on her stomach and then slowly makes her way to her bedroom.

She lies on her back, her hand on her stomach. Then she says to what's growing inside her the same words that she fell asleep to as a child.

"I'm not going to be like her."

And then, "I promise, I'm not going to be like her."

"Mama! Mama! Give me those keys!" yells Cheryl, fourteen and scared shitless.

Mama can hardly speak, but she wants the keys to meet her boyfriend at the bar. Her friend Joan just called and said he was chatting up some dumb bitch. Cheryl-Lee thought Mama was due for a night in of drinking and passing out, so she'd sat herself at the dining room table trying to get some schoolwork done. But when Mama got the phone call, Cheryl-Lee knew she would have to hide the keys. But Mama was swift on her feet tonight, emboldened by rage and jealousy.

"Fuck off, Cheryl-Lee!" Mama yells at the top of her lungs. The neighbours can hear, Cheryl is sure, but she doesn't have time to feel humiliated.

"NO! You give them to me right now! You are not driving tonight!"

She moves closer to Mama, trying to find a good way to wrestle them away from her. But she grabs the keys too quickly. Now Mama's got her and isn't letting go.

"Mama! Let go! Mama, Mama, you're hurting me! Let go!" Cheryl-Lee wheezes. She can't breathe.

Mama lets her go. Cheryl-Lee has to take them, she can't let her drive like this. She moves slowly away from Mama and then swings back, grabbing the keys from her hand.

It takes Mama a second to know what's happened, and Cheryl-Lee is already running when Mama grabs her. Mama spins her around and punches her, twice, hard, right in the nose.

Cheryl-Lee brings her hands up to her face to protect herself when she sees red all over. She's bleeding, and it's bad. It's broken, she thinks. It's broken.

She turns around, hand over her nose, and runs up to her room. She locks the door and throws the keys under her pillow. She tries to stop the bleeding with her bedsheet.

The next morning, Mama, hungover but sober, drives Cheryl-Lee to the hospital. They tell the nurses in the ER that she fell. Mama tells her that she's quitting, for good this time.

Cheryl-Lee believes her.

As the years passed, Cheryl realizes that's the most difficult part of being an alcoholic's child.

You believe them, every time. The disappointment hurts more than any broken bone.

And it never heals.

"You are such a pretty girl, Cheryl. I don't know why you need all those tattoos."

It's eleven o'clock. Cheryl's hungover and it's hotter than hell. Lori made her drive to the house to start sorting Mama's things.

Cheryl turns left, without looking. Why bother? No one else is on the road.

"God also gave me free will, right?"

"That's not the point I am making. You are beautiful and you don't need them."

"Here, Lori, this one is religious," says Cheryl, pointing to her bicep, lifting both hands off the wheel.

"That is a skull wearing a top hat smoking a cigarette," says Lori. "Watch the road!"

Cheryl stops the car abruptly. Lori scowls. She parks it by the side of the road.

And we're here, she thinks.

This is worse than I remembered, but I can't back out. The funeral is day after tomorrow. I need to get this done today.

It's a small house, brick, one and a half storeys. The lawn is dry and overgrown by weeds. Cheryl looks in the mailbox. It's full of junk mail and bills. Literal white trash. The gravel driveway leads to the front door.

Here goes nothing, Cheryl thinks as she walks into the house.

"Why is it so dark in here?"

"Shannon liked it dark," says Lori.

She runs her hand over the wooden bookshelf; it's dusty. Filthy. The same poster of John Wayne and some stupid horse is hung on the wall in exactly the same place.

Lori can keep that.

She walks through the front room. It's as if she's walked into a movie set untouched for ten years. Still the same couches, only they're ripped now. A picture of her as a little girl in a pink Goodwill dress on a small scratched table. Cheryl remembers that dress.

"Okay," she says, "let's get this started."

She has no energy to be sentimental. She doesn't want to start remembering things. She just wants to go home.

"I'll start in the kitchen, you want to take the upstairs?" Lori asks.

Cheryl sits in Mama's bedroom on a cardboard box marked ODDS AND ENDS. So far, she's thrown out everything she's found in it.

Clothes, sheets, books, it's all in there. There's not a single thing she wants for herself. She sits on the box, unable to move.

What the fuck am I doing here? she thinks.

How strange it is to sit with everything Mama had, to be surrounded by her things, things she kept her whole life.

Cheryl has seen so many shrinks, talked to so many people, but she could never make sense of why she got the mama she did. Cheryl started being mad and then she got sad. Now she was just numb but always acutely aware of Mama. Cheryl knew Mama was far away, but she felt so near. How could a mama so absent also be so present?

She gets up from the box and looks around the room, deciding what to pack next. She puts her hand on her stomach absently. After a few seconds, she feels movement.

"What the . . ."

Then she remembers.

The baby. Did it kick?

"Lori?" she yells down the stairs.

"Yeah?"

"I'm going out."

Then, after two smokes in rapid succession, she gets in the car and drives away without looking.

"Why can't you forgive her?" asks Ben.

It's springtime, the year they got together. They're happy. As happy as they know how to be.

Cheryl has just started talking to him about Mama, and he's the first person she's ever wanted to be honest with. She thinks she loves him, how she knows to love, anyway. Her heart is inexperienced, not yet worn in like a baseball glove. Not misshapen and sagged. She's tender with him.

"I just . . . can't."

"Do you miss her?"

"I miss what I never had. I've spent my whole life missing something I've never had."

"Do you ever want to forgive her?"

"Yes."

"Then why don't you?"

"Because she's never going to change."

He nods.

After a while, he speaks again, only softer and slower this time.

"I just think that you only have one mom, and one day you're going to wish things were different."

Maybe, she thinks.

"No. I won't."

Maybe, she thinks again.

Maybe.

When Cheryl gets into town she realizes she's starving. She hasn't had a burger in five years, but it's all her body wants. She stops at a roadside Burger Bar, taking in how green everything is. She'd forgotten the green.

She walks into the restaurant. There is Elvis paraphernalia, pictures of 1950s movie stars, and flags everywhere. She sits in a booth near the door. She just wants to eat and get out. She checks her phone.

Ben still hasn't contacted her.

A small older woman, skinny except for an unfortunate potbelly, comes to take her order. That's what I'll look like in a few months, thinks Cheryl before she catches herself.

"What can I get you?"

"A burger."

"Anything else?"

"Fries. Is it too early for a beer?" she asks, then laughs.

The lady laughs back.

"We don't serve."

The lady looks at her and smiles. Then her faces changes.

"Shannon's daughter?" she asks.

"Yes," says Cheryl, not moving.

"Sweet Jesus," says the woman.

"I'm sorry, have we met?"

"No. No, we've never met, but I knew your mom."

"Yeah?"

The lady stares at Cheryl, then catches herself.

"Yeah. Yeah, I'm so sorry for staring. You just look so much like her."

Cheryl feels the walls contracting, inching closer.

"Yeah?" says Cheryl.

"You sound just like her too."

Cheryl can't remember how Mama sounded. She would have sworn that she did, but now that she thinks about it, she can't.

"Well, we both smoke. Or smoked."

The lady sits down in the booth.

"I am just so sorry about Shannon."

"Thanks," says Cheryl. She pretends to be sadder than she is so the lady will think she needs to be left the fuck alone.

"You know, she used to come in here on Saturdays and have all us ladies in the back laughing. She was a card, your mama."

Cheryl smiles, tightlipped.

"When we heard she'd passed, well, we were all just so sad. She was too young, you know. Earl told us it was a heart attack. That's so awful."

That was big of Earl. A heart attack does sound better than drunkenly falling to your own death.

"Yeah, she had a bad heart. Smoking."

Cheryl smiles. This lady isn't going to leave me alone, she thinks.

"I'm sorry, I just feel like I know you. Your mama talked about you so much. What a big-city girl you were. I just heard so much about you I feel like we're friends."

Cheryl's smile tightens.

"Yeah, and how you couldn't come down here because you were so busy with work. I just wish we'd gotten to meet while your mama was still here."

"Yeah, I wish we'd met too."

"We're all going to the service."

Cheryl nods. "Sorry, can I make that onion rings, instead?"

Almost back at the kitchen, the waitress turns to Cheryl. "It's just so good to meet you finally."

"Sure," says Cheryl.

When her food comes, she can't eat it.

Outside, she calls Ben. He doesn't pick up.

Cheryl is back in Mama's bedroom.

She drove back to the house as dusk fell. Lori had already left. There was a note on the door that read, "Let yourself in, dinner in fridge at home if you want it. Earl picked me up. God Bless, Aunt L."

Cheryl took the note off the door, crumpled it, and then threw it with the rest of the mess on the lawn. No way she'll be home for dinner. She promised herself on the drive back that she was going to get all this stuff packed away today, even if it meant staying here all night. Even if it killed her.

"There is no fucking way I'm coming back here tomorrow," she whispers, walking through what Lori's packed up of the kitchen and living room. After the bedroom, there couldn't be much left.

Cheryl decided to go through Mama's top drawers. She'd thrown out all the underwear and socks. She was on the last drawer, filled with scarves. They smelled like cheap perfume. Mama must have worn them when she went out whoring.

She's just about got them all out when she feels something hard and square in the farthest corner of the drawer. She pushes the last few scarves away and grabs envelopes with the name *David* written across the first one.

Who's David?

Then, without thinking, she takes them and sits on Mama's bed.

The first letter is dated May 5, 1976. She looks around the room, scared, then realizes that no one is watching. She puts her head down and reads.

Shannon,
I just read your last letter, and I don't know what to say.
I can't love you. And I don't know why. But I

can't love you how you love me. Not how you want
me to.

Don't leave him. Not for me. Stay with him, let
him be your husband. Don't leave him.

I won't be there waiting for you. I don't know
why. I just know that I can't ask you to.

David.

Cheryl looks back at the date. 1976. She wasn't born, but Mama
and Dad were together.

She flips the page. It's not David's writing anymore. It's a letter
in Mama's writing. One she sent, that he sent back to her. It's dated
three days earlier.

She knows what this letter would say, should say. She doesn't
want to read anymore, but like a witness to a car crash, she can't
look away. She is the passive onlooker, the third party, watching
dumbfounded as they slide toward each other in slow motion.

David,

I hate myself for writing you this. But I have to write
you because I need to know one way or another. I
need to know what's going to happen, in black and
white.

Two years.

I know that I am with Joshua. I know that he
does love me. But I don't love him, not how I love
you. I feel like there is a code written on my heart
and only you can read it. I could carry on forever
just being loved halfway.

I hate what I'm doing to him.

I love you. Tell me what to do.

Shannon.

Cheryl puts the letters down. She can't read anymore. She starts shaking all over.

She gets up off the bed, and without any warning she's sick. All over the floor.

"I need talk to Lori," she says, to whom she's not sure.

"Who is David?" Cheryl asks Lori as soon as she gets in the door. Lori is sitting in the living room, already in her nightgown.

"David who?"

"Mama's David. Who is he? Tell me right now."

Lori looks like she's seen a ghost.

"Why?"

"Because I found the letters."

"What letters?"

"The letters they sent each other. Who is he? Tell me."

Lori turns away, only her profile visible. She looks as if she is in a naked place, frightened and alone.

"Okay," she says finally. "He was a man your mother loved very much."

"Did Dad know?"

"This is why I don't want to be telling you all this. You already think ill of your mother and . . ."

Cheryl opens her mouth to speak, but Lori cuts her off.

"If your father knew, he never spoke about it. I knew. I didn't like David from the beginning. I didn't think it was right. Your daddy was a good person and he loved Shannon. And in some ways, she did love your daddy, but not . . ."

"But not how she loved David?"

"No. Never how she loved David. More than I think people should love. It was scary almost."

Every word goes through Cheryl like a bullet, the hot metal melting away her skin, leaving her organs exposed.

"What happened?"

"They got together, you know, after meeting at work. At some bar in town. Your mama didn't plan it. She told me once it was like she had no say, no control, no choice, and she was thrown into something head first, and before she could blink, they were heavily involved."

"Did she want to leave Daddy for him?"

Aunt Lori brings her hands to her face, sucks in her lips, tight, and doesn't move.

"Forgive me," she whispers.

She looks at Cheryl. "She was really torn up about it."

"What does that mean?"

"I think she would have. But she loved your father, she did. She was just complicated, you know. He put up with a lot from her. He didn't understand her, but he did love her. Your mama wished that she could love him the same too, I know she did."

Cheryl loved her father because he wasn't complicated. He loved her back, but he never really knew her. They were like two differed breeds, existing in different orbits, pretending they breathed the same air.

"What was David like?"

"Handsome. Dynamic. Different from your father. I hated him from the moment I met him, but it wasn't easy."

"What did he look like?"

"Dark-haired. Very tall. He had a breadth to him, he was strong-looking. Blue eyes. There's a picture of him, upstairs in the hall, with your mama and I in it. Next to the bible verse. I keep it up because she looks so happy."

Cheryl's body grows suddenly cold, her blood evaporating.

"He was magnetic. Funny, smart, stubborn. He wanted a lot more than this town had to offer. He was strange, though. There was something bad that surrounded him."

Lori looks down, a new sadness shaping her features.

"He was a lot like Shannon," she says privately.

"So what ended up happening?"

"When she married your daddy, she stopped seeing him. I know she did, she changed after that. It was like a light was sucked out of her. She changed altogether after she stopped seeing him."

"Really?"

"He ruined her."

I don't want to be ruined, thinks Cheryl. Please, she prays, don't let me be spoilt.

"It was him that did it? You believe that?" asks Cheryl, feeling bound. She doesn't really want to know the answer.

"I think, I think she had a hand in it. But she was weak. I think it was just bad luck that they ever met. Because I don't think she could control it. I think it got so big, so heavy, that she could never get out from under it."

"But she did leave him? Eventually, she left him?"

"Physically, she left him. But if you want to know the truth, I think she loved him until her heart stopped."

"Do you know where I could find him?"

Lori looks winded.

Cheryl found him in the phone book. David Hawco. He owns a small gas station.

"Yeah?" he said when he picked up the phone.

His voice was slow and rough, and even though Cheryl knew they've never met, she swore she'd heard it before. He felt so familiar.

"Hi, ah, I have a problem with my windshields. I was hoping I could come in."

There was a pause on the other end. She could hear him shuffling papers.

"How's 2:25?"

"Good."

"See you then," he said. She held the phone to her ear for a full two minutes after he'd hung up.

When she finally put it down, she was left wondering if closeness could be transferred through DNA. If that kind of love was passed on, through you, despite all the pain, the anger, and loneliness it created in you. If it lived forever, even if all you wanted was for it to die.

Cheryl is in her car, outside the garage. It's boiling out, but she feels suddenly cold. She turns off her air conditioner. She undoes her window and breaths deeply.

It's 2:20. Five more minutes, she thinks. Don't worry, there is still five more minutes.

She wishes she'd had another drink before she left.

She flips down the visor above her. She looks at herself in the mirror.

Her makeup is too thick, she thinks. She was nervous and she put on too much. She finds a used tissue and wipes it away. But her touch is too rough, and her face feels tender. She puts the tissue down, now coloured and torn.

She sees a man, a silver-haired man, walk out of the garage.

Has to be David.

He lights a smoke. He walks closer to her but stops halfway between where she's parked and the front door of the shop. He doesn't see her, she's certain.

He stands, tall and proud. His face looks worn. There are other people milling around him, but no one talks to him. Even with people surrounding, he's alone.

He takes a few more drags and then throws the cigarette away. There is a hostility in his movements. Then, as if he can feel her watching him, he turns. Now they are staring at each other. His face moves, and he looks spooked. She's certain he's seen her. Then he walks toward her.

"Cheryl-Lee?"

How does he know my name?

"Cheryl-Lee?" he asks again.

"It's Cheryl now."

His face is so clear to her, it's like someone took a permanent marker and outlined every feature in his face. His eyes are the same colour as the turquoise stone around his neck. He won't take them off her and she can't look away, even though he hurts to look at.

"You're not here for your car."

"I'll be back tomorrow," David yelled to a black guy working the desk inside the garage. The only black guy Cheryl's seen since leaving the city.

They left as quickly as they could but didn't speak until they were far away from everyone else, captured by the fear of being over-heard. Why does this already feel so secretive? Cheryl wondered.

He seems so nervous.

"I'm not here to tell you that you're my father, don't worry."

He looks at her and smiles. His face is so different when he smiles. "I already know that, girl."

They are seated and smoking. Mel's, like everywhere else in Wellington, has not yet complied with twenty-first-century smoking bylaws. They reach for the menu at the same time and their hands brush ever so slightly.

"How do you know me?" she asks because she can't think of anything else to say.

"We've met."

"What?"

"A couple of times. She brought you to see me when you were a little baby, but you wouldn't remember that. I knocked on your door one time asking for her, and you told me she wasn't home. You must've been about fifteen. You looked so much like her . . . like when I first met her. I guess I frightened you with all the staring because you told me 'Take a picture, it lasts longer' and then slammed the door in my face."

"Sorry."

"It's all right."

Cheryl can't remember the meeting. Must have been a couple of months before she left home. Things were so bad she's purposefully forgotten everything that happened around then. She has forced whole years out of her head and is proud of it.

"I would see you around town, and I would try not to stare but the resemblance was something shocking. Still is."

"People keep telling me that."

"It's a compliment."

"Not to me."

A waitress comes, and they order coffees and pie.

"Then one day, I just stopped seeing you."

"I left."

"Your mom told me."

When?

"How often did you two speak?"

"Almost never. But we spoke a lot when we did."

"Lori told me you stopped speaking."

"We stopped being what we were. But we would never have stopped speaking. Not possible. We converse in my head all the time."

They both laugh but briefly, spooked.

"So, how is she?"

"Mama?"

"Yeah."

Oh, fuck.

"You don't know?"

"Know what?"

Oh, fuck.

"She died."

His face stops. His pupils widen and his irises become bluer than they were a second ago, bluer than any blue she's ever seen. She wants to look away, but she can't.

"When?" he whispers.

"Last week. Funeral's tomorrow."

He nods.

"What happened?"

"She fell. No one was there to help her."

"Was she drinking?" he asks.

Cheryl says she doesn't know, suddenly self-conscious that he can smell the alcohol on her breath.

"I'm sorry. How did you not know?"

He nods again.

"I don't have a lot of friends," he says.

"I never knew about you until last night. I found the letters you sent each other—I asked Lori who you were."

"After talking to Lori you must think I'm a pretty bad guy."

"I'm just pretty fucked up right now. You were a big part of her, a big part that I never knew about."

He looks down and fiddles with a ring on his finger.

He's married.

"Look, you gotta know that if she was alive I wouldn't tell you anything."

"Okay."

He looks up at her again. Somewhere, she's known these eyes, in an unsayable way, her whole life.

"So what do you wanna know?"

"Well . . . I guess, when was the last time you saw her?"

"A year, a year and a half ago. Shannon and I, it didn't matter if we didn't see each other for ten years, I'd see her again and nothing had changed."

"So what does your wife think about that?"

He doesn't flinch.

"I'm not apologizing to you. You get old and being alone's not so desirable as it once was."

"Did Mama know?"

He nods.

"So . . . is it true that you stopped being together? Or were you always . . . together? Like when my dad was around?"

"We were never really . . . I was young and I was mean. But we stopped sleeping together when she married your father."

He sighs so heavily that Cheryl can feel his weight all over her.

"Being with your mother felt like home, but not in a good way. Not everybody likes home. Sometimes that comfort can make you all the more uncomfortable."

"How so?" Cheryl asks, but she has the sickening feeling that she knows exactly how and so.

The coffees and pie arrive. He waits until the waitress leaves.

"I never had anything like that with anyone but your mother. We knew each other on our insides. I don't think people should know each other like that. I did bad things to her."

The way he speaks, the way he moves, the violence in his eyes, he is so much like Ben.

"The best sense I can make of it is that we were both as drawn to each other as we were repelled. I loved her, but it never hurt me to hurt her. Sometimes I would force myself to try, to try to love her right, but I never could."

"Do you regret it?" she asks for herself.

He doesn't move.

"I'm just trying to be honest. I'm not proud of how I was."

Cheryl nods.

They both eat their pie in silence.

"Was she different when you two were together?"

"Somewhere I think people are always who they are and there's no changing them."

"So she was always bad?"

"She was helpless." He looks so sorry for her.

He can see that helplessness in me, she thinks. Soon she hates looking at him more than she's ever hated anything, but she can't look away. Cheryl feels a wetness down her face. Her heart has crept up her chest and is beating in her throat.

"You should have helped her, David."

He looks at his coffee. Cheryl feels like a rope has been cut between them, and she can look down again now. She grabs a napkin and wipes her face. Then the sick rising. I have to leave, she thinks. He looks up at her again.

"You know the strange thing?" he says.

"What?" Cheryl says, scared to look up.

"I thought I saw her yesterday."

About ten minutes later she's in her car, leaving. He told her to come find him anytime she needed. When they were saying good-bye, he put his hands on her cheeks, holding her face. His hands were so rough, and she knew it wasn't her he was trying to reach.

She had never seen anyone look as sad when he let her go.

Cheryl is lying in bed, on her back. Her hand is on her stomach.

Her mother's funeral is tomorrow. The black dress is hanging on her door, the jewellery is laid out, the heaven and heaviness of life passing over lying next to her.

She says to what's growing inside her the same words that she fell asleep to as a child.

"I'm not going to be like her."

Then, "I'm not going to be like her."

And then, "I promise, I'm not going to be like her."

Acknowledgments

I'd like to thank my mother for encouraging me. I'd like to thank my father for helping me, always. I'd like to thank my brother for inspiring me. I'd like to thank my sister for her strength. I'd like to thank my agents Anne McDermid and Monica Pacheco for being so supportive and believing in me. I would like to thank Ruth Linka at Brindle & Glass for wanting to publish this book, helping this collection find a home. I'd like to thank my editor Lynne Van Luven for her tireless work and patience; you have improved this book tenfold. And finally, I'd like to thank Caroline Leavitt for being a perfect mentor.

KATIE BOLAND is an actress and writer who divides her time between Los Angeles and Toronto. She was chosen as one of the Toronto International Film Festival's "Rising Stars" and as one of three Canadians to watch by *Elle Canada*. She has appeared in more than forty films and her writing has appeared in the *Toronto Star* and *TChad Quarterly*. *Eat Your Heart Out* is her first published work. Please visit Katie online at katieboland.com, @katieboland, or on her blog, comedy-and-drama.blogspot.com.